Royal Sarala Weddings

Can these royal siblings find their perfect match?

Prince Rohan of Sarala has always known of the responsibility he was born into—destined to one day be king, but it hasn't stopped him from being a little rebellious! While his older sister, Princess Marisa, has always been accepting of her kingdom's long-standing traditions, it doesn't mean she agrees with them! But now it's time for them to step up and marry... Is it possible to tame the Sarala siblings?

Don't miss these fabulous books from Nina Milne!

His Princess on Paper

When Prince Rohan meets his suitably arranged fiancée, Elora, from a neighboring island, he's shocked by the very undeniable and mutual chemistry he was *not* expecting! Maybe a convenient engagement can also be fun...?

Available now!

Bound by Their Royal Baby

Princess Marisa of Sarala was never meant to take the throne. But when she discovers her one night with a perfectly delectable stranger has resulted in a pregnancy, suddenly *everything* in her life is about to change...forever!

Coming soon!

Dear Reader,

I really enjoyed writing Elora and Rohan's story—
partly because I set it on a fictional Indian island, and
it was fun to imagine that, but also because I loved
taking them from the perspective that they were only
together out of a deep sense of duty and emotional
obligation to the end, where they truly loved each
other and wanted to be together with every fiber of
their beings.

I hope you enjoy reading how they got there.

Nina x

His Princess
on Paper

Nina Milne

HARLEQUIN

Romance

Recycling programs
for this product may
not exist in your area.

ISBN-13: 978-1-335-59663-5

His Princess on Paper

Copyright © 2024 by Nina Milne

For questions and comments about the quality of this book,
please contact us at CustomerService@Harlequin.com.

TM and ® are trademarks of Harlequin Enterprises ULC.

Harlequin Enterprises ULC
22 Adelaide St. West, 41st Floor
Toronto, Ontario M5H 4E3, Canada
www.Harlequin.com

Printed in U.S.A.

Nina Milne has always dreamed of writing for Harlequin Romance—ever since she played libraries with her mother's stacks of Harlequin romances as a child. On her way to this dream, Nina acquired an English degree, a hero of her own, three gorgeous children and—somehow!—an accountancy qualification. She lives in Brighton and has filled her house with stacks of books—her very own *real* library.

Books by Nina Milne

Harlequin Romance

The Casseveti Inheritance

Italian Escape with the CEO
Whisked Away by the Italian Tycoon
The Secret Casseveti Baby

The Christmas Pact

Snowbound Reunion in Japan

Baby on the Tycoon's Doorstep
Second Chance in Sri Lanka
Falling for His Stand-In Fiancée
Consequence of Their Dubai Night
Wedding Planner's Deal with the CEO

Visit the Author Profile page
at Harlequin.com for more titles.

To my grandmother (Mamama) and my mum,
for both being such fun, good, loving grandmothers

Praise for
Nina Milne

CHAPTER ONE

HIS ROYAL HIGHNESS PRINCE ROHAN, unwilling heir to the Kingdom of Sarala, glanced around the small cargo plane as it landed on the tiny, mostly disused airfield and then turned to smile at the pilot.

'Thank you, Amit, old friend. I appreciate the lift. And the privacy.'

'Any time, Ro. And good luck. If you need a quick escape, you know where to find me.'

The words, though said half in jest, had an uncomfortable element of truth—there was a chance, slim but there, that Rohan would need an escape route. Not just him, but the whole royal family of Sarala. If Sarala decided to copy the almost unprecedented step that its neighbouring island of Baluka had taken—and declare itself a republic, deposing the incumbent royal family.

As if sensing his friend's thoughts, Amit shook his head. 'It'll be all right, Ro. I've spoken to my family, to other people, and they don't want Sarala to become a republic. They're happy with the status quo, and with your parents. They are good, just rulers who look after the island and the people. Sarala is mostly prosperous and peaceful—why rock the boat?'

Rohan smiled at his childhood friend, son of the palace head gardener and one of the very few people on Sarala who treated him like a normal human being, not a prince. 'I don't think it's my parents who are the problem. I think it's the next generation.' He shook his head. 'No, that's not fair.' His older sister, Marisa, wasn't at fault, after all he was the heir. 'It's me.'

He closed his eyes for a moment, recalled exactly why the people saw him as a problem, remembered the glare of publicity, the relentless coverage of the breakdown of his disastrous marriage, the descriptions of him as 'cold', 'brutal', 'heartless'—a bridegroom wedded to duty, a frozen-hearted prince with no sympathy for his 'persecuted bride'. The photos of his then wife, Princess Caro, tears in her wide green eyes, anguish etched on every beautiful feature.

The memories streamed through his brain and triggered the searing sensation of remembered humiliation, the deep tearing wound of betrayal. But the humiliation, the pain, he had at least been able to keep private—not one person knew the truth of his marriage and none ever would.

He opened his eyes, saw his friend's expression of sympathy. Amit had no idea what had really happened but he would be able to guess how much Rohan had loathed the public analysis of his private life. The whispers and rumours, the swirling speculation, the hidden conversations and sideways looks.

Now he spoke. 'Maybe it's time to fix that, put the past behind you. Spend some more time on Sarala, show the people what you're really made of.'

Problem was, Rohan wasn't sure what he was made of, other than flesh, blood, bone and other wobbly bits, just like anyone else. And he couldn't see why that would impress the people, who had already judged him. That was why he had left Sarala; his parents had been adamant it was the only way to kill the scandal once the divorce was finalised and he'd been forced to agree, despite the uncomfortable sense that it looked as though he were fleeing.

So he had spent the last three years abroad as Sarala's ambassador, and whilst doing that he'd made a new life for himself, a life he loved—one that had now been upended by his recall to Sarala. An unwelcome recall, but he accepted the necessity. He closed his eyes, hoping against hope that this was a temporary necessity, suspected deep down that it wouldn't be.

'I'm not sure they'll like what they see,' he told Amit now.

'That depends what you decide to show them,' his friend said somewhat cryptically, but before Rohan could ask what he meant Amit glanced down at his phone. 'I've asked a friend of mine, Jamal, to pick you up and take you to the palace. Someone I trust,' Amit continued. 'He's there now.'

A few minutes later Rohan stepped onto the tarmac of the tiny airport, relieved to see that there was no waiting fanfare, no reporters here to record the returning son. Relieved that Amit's trust in his friend wasn't misplaced—there had been no tipoff to the press. He glanced around and headed towards the small, discreet dark car parked in the shadows and climbed into the passenger seat.

'Good evening, Your Highness.' The young man sounded nervous and Rohan smiled quickly, even as he wished his royalty didn't affect people.

'No need for formality. Please call me Rohan.'

The young man in the driving seat looked surprised but nodded, before executing a faultless turn and making his way to the main road, as Rohan assessed the mirrors, checking for signs of pursuit or interest.

'I don't think anyone can know that I am giving you a lift. I told no one.'

'I appreciate that.' He glanced at Jamal's serious expression. 'I don't want to cause any unrest or a stir until I have a chance to speak with my parents.' Speaking of whom, it was time to let them know what was going on, now it was too late for them to arrange a ceremonious welcome, if that was what they had planned. He messaged them.

Change of plan. My flight arrived this evening and I am headed to the palace now.

Jamal nodded. 'I understand.'

There was silence after that and Rohan looked out at the dusky night sky, the indigo darkness of a Saralan night, inhaled the familiar scent of lush sweet flowers that wafted in through the open windows. The smell of home, and for an instant he wished he could be here anonymously, could simply come and go unseen. Or at least only be seen when he chose to be seen.

Instead, he watched as the imposing gates, set in the vast stretch of whitewashed walls that surrounded the palace of Sarala, loomed ahead.

'I'll walk the last bit,' he told Jamal, not wanting to expose this young man to the security officers who would be patrolling. 'I'll get in via a side entrance. And thank you.'

'You're welcome. Amit speaks highly of you and I am glad to have met you.'

'You too.'

Ten minutes later, he approached the side entrance, where he was met by a stiff-faced guard. 'The King and Queen are expecting you in the Throne Room.'

Of course they were. The Throne Room, with its long mahogany table, its dazzling gilt-edged throne, the paintings on the wall of former rulers, the ancient tapestries woven from the silk for which Sarala was justly famed, the room where formal negotiations were carried out, visiting dignitaries met to display and be awed by the weight of royalty, the evidence of the dynasty of the Kamodian family.

So this was to be *that* sort of meeting—the return of Prince Rohan, Ambassador for Sarala, not a family welcome. Well, what had he expected?

Rohan loved his parents, he did, and they loved him. But he knew that for them the most important thing, the thing they loved the most, was Sarala, and this meeting would be about Sarala.

'I will call for someone to take you there.'

'There is no need. I know the way.' Yet his footsteps lagged as he scrunched across the gravel driveway, heard the rhythmic flow and fall of the water feature, and saw the dimly illuminated shapes of the hedges and bushes of the landscaped garden. For an absurd moment he looked up at the sky, in the foolish hope that Amit would swoop down in his plane and essay a rescue. But the dusky Saralan sky showed only the glitter of stars and the curve of the moon.

He entered via a side entrance and made his way down the long marble corridors of the palace to the throne room. Opened the door to see his parents at the table that stretched across the marble floor, and he looked from the two thrones on a dais across to the stained-glass windows that depicted kings of yesteryear.

King Hanuman and Queen Kaamini rose and stepped up onto the dais in front of the thrones and he joined them, knelt for the traditional blessing.

'Amma, Papa,' he murmured and then stood and waited as his parents returned to the table, sat and then motioned for him to follow suit.

His parents' eyes rested on him and he could see the hint of approbation, the searching glances, the disapproval at his attire—jeans and a T-shirt.

His father's voice, though, was measured. 'It is good to see you, my son. But we would have preferred a more official arrival.'

'Your message said you wished for my urgent return. Given the situation with Baluka, I thought it made more sense to arrive unofficially.'

'Well, the important thing is that you are here.

And here to stay. Your mother and I are recalling you to Sarala. Permanently. It is time for the heir to return home. Time to show the people that you are ready to settle down and learn to rule.'

The words sat like cold stones in his belly. Even though he'd known this would come—had known it all his life.

'You have done good work in the past few years and been an excellent ambassador for your country. Now it is time to show that you are capable of being a prince and a ruler. To do your duty.'

The weight of that duty, the mantle of royalty, seemed to descend on his shoulders. A duty he'd been born to and would carry out. Because he did love his country, this exotic, lush, beautiful island, producer of the finest silk in the world. And if he wished he'd been born a mere citizen rather than a prince it was a wish that was futile and pointless. And he understood that. If he wished the law could be changed to reflect modern times and allow Marisa, older than he by two years, to be heir, he knew better than to voice that wish.

But he could at least try to buy some time.

'I understand you wish me to be here more, but I would prefer not to leave my recent duties as ambassador incomplete.' Didn't want to leave the life he'd made—more importantly, the business he'd built. His business, one his parents were unaware of.

'There are more important duties now,' his mother said. 'It is time to provide Sarala with an heir. That is why you will marry.'

'No.' The denial came from deep within; he couldn't—wouldn't—make the same mistake twice.

Both parents raised their eyebrows in a synchronised movement that would have been comical at any other moment than this.

'I am not ready,' Rohan said. Not now, not ever.

'This is not about you. The kingdom needs an heir, needs continuity, needs certainty. A ruler who is here and present, taking no risks, and who has sons to follow him.' His father's voice was even and brooked no refusal.

The Queen continued. 'The monarchy on Baluka fell because there was no heir. Just a distant cousin many times removed who the people did not want. And so they stormed the palace and the King and Queen had to flee.' There was outrage in her voice, but also a thread of fear, one that touched Rohan with sympathy, even as a visceral, raw panic assailed him. A cold sense of inevitability. Yet he tried.

'I do understand, Amma, and in time…'

'There is no time. The preparations are already

in hand,' his mother continued. 'Tomorrow you will meet your bride.'

Rohan stared at his parents, opened his mouth to protest.

'This is not about what you want; it is about what Sarala needs,' King Hanuman said, his voice deep with emotion and a certainty that his son would understand. 'This is about your duty.'

The following morning

Her Royal Highness Princess Elora of Caruli stared at her reflection, amazed that the years of training were still holding good, that somehow her countenance retained a serene expression, when inside, anxiety, nerves and panic fought for victory.

Somehow, she was even managing to focus on her mother's words, perhaps in the vain hope that Queen Joanna was going to tell her this whole thing was a joke. That she *wasn't* about to meet Prince Rohan, that there was no question of marriage.

Panic swirled and soared again. How could she marry Prince Rohan when the very idea filled her with cold dread?

Perhaps her mother sensed her turmoil. 'Elora. You understand the importance of this meeting. You must please Prince Rohan, show him you will be a worthy bride. This marriage is necessary and you will do your duty.' The words were a statement, not a question, uttered in the cold, distant tones she recognised so well, ever since the death of her twin brother. How she wished Sanjay was still here now, that he'd grown up alongside her. 'This is your chance to do something for your country.'

The word *finally*, though unsaid, seemed to hover in the air, flashing neon.

'I understand.' And she did; an alliance between Sarala and Caruli was vital for both islands now that Baluka had declared itself a republic. For centuries the three neighbouring islands had veered from friendship to enmity until in recent decades they had settled to a civilised alliance of sorts. Uneasy sometimes but an alliance.

But, of course, now everything would change and no doubt Sarala was as shaken as Caruli by events. And so her parents and Rohan's parents had come up with this. A way of joining forces.

A marriage to tie the royal families of the two islands together. No matter the idea filled her with terror—marriage to Rohan, the prince who had already driven one wife away, resulting in a divorce that had fuelled public speculation for years.

'Elora.' Her mother's voice was tart. 'Are you listening?'

'Yes, Mama. And I do understand.'

'Then make sure you impress on Rohan that this marriage must take place. Soon.' The older woman's perfectly made-up face scrunched into a frown of disapproval. 'It is ridiculous that he has insisted on seeing you alone. Make sure you say nothing wrong, show him what a good future queen you will make. A future queen and mother to his heir. Because there has to be an heir, Elora. A son.'

Elora tried to keep her face serene, her body relaxed. Marriage did indeed involve more than a political alliance. As for getting an heir, her mother, of all people, knew that it wasn't that easy. Queen Joanna had tried for years, undergone secret fertility treatment until finally the miracle had happened and an heir had been born. Along with Elora—an unnecessary addition to the family but tolerated, loved even, until Sanjay's death.

What if pregnancy wasn't that easy for Elora either? There could be inherited problems; her mother knew that. Knew too that Elora's periods were irregular.

'I can't guarantee that. Perhaps it is better to tell the Saralan royal family now about...'

'No.' Her mother's voice was sharp and she

glanced around as though the walls were sprouting proverbial ears. 'There is nothing to tell. Within a year you will have a son. I am sure of it. You will be like your sister.'

Elora held her tongue, didn't point out that Flavia was her half-sister. Flavia was the King's daughter from his first marriage to Queen Matilda, who he had divorced in order to marry Elora's mother, Queen Joanna.

Flavia had lived with her mother until Sanjay's tragic death had left Caruli without an heir. Once it had become clear that there would be no more children from Queen Joanna, Flavia had been recalled to the palace. Not because she could inherit, but because it had become imperative that she marry and produce an heir. Which she had duly and dutifully done, and now her son Viraj was five years old and heir to Caruli.

Now it was Elora's turn to duly, dutifully marry to produce an heir for Sarala. She understood that, but what if she was unable to carry out her duty in full?

'But perhaps we should at least have some tests done.' Her words were tentative; questioning her mother was not something to be undertaken lightly.

'No.' The reply was sharp, bringing back memories of other sharp words—words of censure, words that had caused pain, however much Elora knew she deserved them. 'There is no need and if anyone found out, rumours would fly. You are creating problems unnecessarily.' There was a slight pause and her mother gripped her arm. 'You have caused enough damage.' The words were said so softly it took Elora a second to absorb them, their meaning impacting with a dull, agonising thud even as the Queen continued. 'Do not do more. Then one day Flavia's son will rule Caruli and your son will rule Sarala.'

Now the Queen smiled, a frosty smile but a smile nonetheless, and it was a balm for Elora, and a promise that perhaps one day she would see the mother she remembered from when Sanjay was alive. A mother who had smiled often, and if that smile had mostly been for her brother there had still been leftover warmth and diluted love for Elora.

Perhaps she could win some of it back. By doing her duty. Perhaps she *was* worrying too much, making a problem where none existed.

'Enough talk,' her mother said now. 'I will take you to the meeting room. Remember, Elora, behave with decorum. Show him that you will be a good, dutiful wife.'

Good. Dutiful. Was that what his first wife had pledged to be? Princess Caroline—so vital, so beautiful, so talented and then so tragic.

Elora took one last look at her reflection.

Long blonde hair, carefully clipped up into a
tidy, sleek, glossy chignon. Dressed in a lehenga,
the long, full silk skirt the teal blue of the Carulian flag, embossed with a pale pink diamond
pattern and topped with a short, cropped blouse,
lavishly embroidered, her bare midriff and arms
artfully covered by a gauzy teal chiffon scarf.
Her skin enhanced with the slightest tint of pink
so that she didn't look deathly pale. She knew
she burned too easily, her looks unusual for this
island, courtesy of some European ancestor and
her mother's English ancestry. Grey eyes a swirl
of emotion, and she closed them in a rapid set
of blinks to clear them, dug her nails into the
palms of her hands to ground herself and keep
the growing anxiety at bay.

'I'm ready,' she said.

CHAPTER TWO

ELORA FOCUSED ON taking one step at a time, heading for the Treasure Room, where she was to meet Rohan; her parents had chosen the venue, presumably to remind Prince Rohan that Caruli had just as much treasure as Sarala. With each step, her feet, clad in light embroidered slippers, felt as though they were encased in lead. But still she kept going, told herself that was the only way forward literally. And there was no other direction she could go. This meeting was inevitable, unavoidable. She was doing this for her country. One foot forward. Focus on getting the walk right, demonstrate the grace and poise expected of a Princess of Caruli.

If she kept that focus, she would be able to press down the anxiety that swirled inside her, the currents darker and stronger than the usual everyday nerves she'd learnt to live with. As always, she imagined the barrier holding it down, holding it at bay. An iron bar of control. Because if she allowed that barrier to yield she'd lose it, would show her weakness.

She could never let that happen again; it had been her weakness, her fears that had led to Sanjay's death—Elora could never forget that. Never forget and never forgive herself.

One more graceful step and they reached the Treasure Room, where a staff member waited to push the heavy wooden door open.

Once inside, Queen Joanna looked around the room then turned to the staff member. 'The room has been checked?'

'Yes, Your Majesty. By three different people, including Mr Ashok.'

At the mention of the palace's security officer, Elora knew that her mother had been making sure there were no recording devices in the room, no possibility of a reporter having somehow infiltrated the palace.

The Queen nodded in dismissal. 'Please be sure to tell Prince Rohan this before you bring him here.'

Elora tried to calm her breathing, allowed herself one clench of her fists, dug her perfectly manicured nails into her palms. Nails painted a nice, neutral pale pearl colour that wouldn't call attention but would garner approval at their perfection.

She dug them in hard, needing the pain to

distract her. Looked around the room as well, knowing she needed something to focus on, so if she felt the situation slip from her grasp she could find something to ground her. What better than the portrait of her brother Sanjay, aged eleven, painted just weeks before the fatal accident? After all, nothing could ground her more than the memory of her twin, the ache of missing him still so raw the pain seared her.

She saw that her mother too was looking at the portrait and a wave of sympathy engulfed Elora; her mother's pain at least equalled her own. The loss of her precious son, the heir she'd produced after so much grief and hope.

'Mama…' she began, but wished she hadn't as the Queen turned to her and Elora almost recoiled at the look in her mother's eyes, the flare of cold dislike.

'Do your duty, Elora, and do not make a mess of this. This marriage is necessary.'

And a redemption. Perhaps a way to alleviate her mother's deep, abiding disappointment that it was Sanjay who had died instead of Elora.

But now her heart started to beat faster as the heavy door swung open. To her surprise, it wasn't the equerry who entered, to precede and announce the arrival of the Prince.

Instead, a man she had no difficulty in recognising entered—a man she had briefly encountered years ago at official events, though mostly from a distance as political relations had been going through a strained period. A man she recognised more from the various articles and media posts she'd read.

But the pictures hadn't prepared her for the reality of him now in the flesh. Rohan was tall, his thick dark hair cut short but with a spiky uplift that suggested it was tamed from a tendency to wildness. His face was chiselled, the brown eyes, so dark as to be almost black, held an assurance and a coldness that made Elora shiver.

But it was a shiver caused by something else as well, something she was unable to define, causing her to grip the edge of the nearby chair, making her study him feature by feature. A face that looked etched in marble, all hard lines. The jaw was determined, the nose an aquiline jut—the only thing that looked out of control was the thick dark hair.

For an instant she was aware of his lightning scrutiny and something jolted in his eyes, the coldness charged with a flash of…heat, of surprise, arrest… Elora wasn't sure as it vanished as swiftly as it had arisen and he stepped forward towards her mother.

'Your Majesty.'

The Queen was frowning. 'I apologise for my

equerry. He was instructed to bring you and announce you.'

'Please don't blame him. I prefer to announce myself; I made that clear to him. I would also like to thank you for agreeing that this meeting could be in private.'

Elora managed to restrain herself from an unladylike and audible gulp of shock. His words had been perfectly polite but insistent and the slightly dismissive tone had been unmistakable. If her mother had had any plans of remaining as chaperone they were being thwarted. But he'd had the grace at least to ensure there was no staff member present to witness any possible skirmish.

The Queen gave a regal inclination of her head. 'Your gratitude is noted. Please do not abuse the trust we have put in you. We will see you before you leave.'

'Of course.'

Elora watched as her mother left the room, glanced quickly at the picture of her brother, turned to face Rohan and waited in silence.

'I thought it would be better if our first meeting was in private.' His voice was deep, courteous but hard.

'As you wish,' she murmured. 'I am pleased to meet you again.'

'Are you?'

The question startled her and her eyes widened as she met his gaze, saw the sardonic rise of his eyebrow.

'You can be honest, Elora. That's why I wanted this meeting to be unchaperoned. Without convention and fanfare.' He glanced around. 'Shall we sit?' he suggested, his tone brusque, the words a statement rather than a question, and for a moment she was tempted to refuse, say she would prefer to conduct the conversation standing.

But that would be counter-productive, not what a dutiful wife would do. Plus she would rather be seated. So, without further comment, she headed to the two chairs arranged around an antique table placed in front of the ancient sword, its silver blade gleaming in the sunlight that streamed through the windows, causing the rubied hilt to gleam blood-red, displayed on a table draped with the Carulian flag.

Rohan eyed the sword before sitting. 'The sword that apparently slayed one of my ancestors,' he said.

'Centuries ago,' she replied. 'Isn't there a jewel-hilted dagger in the Throne Room of Sarala?'

'There is. I believe peace was eventually restored back then through marriage.'

'So, hundreds of years ago, a prince and princess sat together like this—maybe times haven't changed as much as all that.'

'All those years ago, that prince and princess had no choice; they were bringing years of bloodshed to an end. We do have a choice. You have a choice. That is what I am here to say. To ask. Are you being forced into this marriage?'

The direct question took her by surprise and she hoped she managed to conceal it as she tried to work out the best answer, found herself buying time with an apparent assumption of innocence. 'Is that a proposal?'

Elora took some satisfaction from seeing that the answer had wrongfooted him, and his lips relaxed into a near semblance of a smile. Suddenly she could almost see the prince who had graced the covers of various celeb publications in the past three years, recently with his arm around a beautiful woman.

Almost. Before his brown eyes hardened once more.

'No, it's not,' he said. 'It's a question. One I'd like a straight answer to.'

Elora paused, considered her options and saw the impatient movement of his fingers as they drummed the side of the chair.

'It's simple enough. Yes or no?'

'It's not that simple,' she snapped, then realised the tartness of her voice and drew a breath. But he wanted honesty, didn't he? 'If you want a single syllable answer, then no. I am not being forced.'

After all, her parents couldn't drag her kicking and screaming to the altar; there was no question of force. Unless the force of duty counted. Or the force of hope—the hope of redemption. The hope that if she did this, she could in some way make up for the death of her brother, for being the twin who had lived. If this marriage meant her parents could show her some forgiveness, some warmth, could be proud of her, then that hope would propel her to the altar.

He studied her expression for a moment then nodded and she took the opportunity to speak. 'Now can I ask you a question?'

'Of course.'

'Do you *want* to marry me?' He opened his mouth and she raised a hand. 'A straight answer, please. Of one syllable.'

That made him pause and now he did smile, a real smile that changed his whole expression and stance, warmed the brown eyes as he looked at her. Really looked at her, and there was that funny little shiver again.

'Touché,' he said.

'You mean it's not that simple?' she asked with exaggerated emphasis. 'You either do or you don't.'

'I don't want to marry anyone,' he stated.

'Then that includes me and the simple answer to the question is no.'

'Only you're right. It's not that simple,' he said.

'Isn't it?' she asked. 'If you don't want to marry me, why are you even here?'

Anxiety threatened and it was an effort to keep her voice steady. If Rohan decided not to go ahead with this marriage her parents would never believe it wasn't her fault. Maybe it would be. But… it would also free her from marriage to a man she didn't know and, from all she'd heard of him, didn't even want to know. A man whose visage was now grim, lips set in a firm line, brown eyes cold.

'Because, as I said, this isn't personal. I have no wish for marriage but I accept that it is a necessity. The dynasty must continue. As such, a marriage to a Princess of Caruli makes sense, given the political situation. As, most likely, our predecessors figured out.'

Sadness and a sense of bleakness touched her even as she appreciated the honest assessment of the situation.

'So perhaps I should change my answer to yes. I do want to marry you.'

The sadness intensified as she wondered what it would be like to be loved for oneself, wanted for herself, not because she was a Princess of Caruli.

'And you?' he asked. 'What of you? Do you want to marry me?'

The words seemed to rush through her head, so portentous she wasn't sure she could even breathe. Marry him. Marry a man who did not love her, did not even like her or know her. Marry a man whose first wife had run from him, and who had since been linked with at least two other women, both beautiful celebrities, as Princess Caro herself had been.

'Like you, I accept the necessity of a marriage.' The words sounded stilted and forced, even to her own ears. For a moment the future stretched before her, bleak and grey—life with a man who believed in duty, a cold man who was marrying her through necessity. As she was marrying him, she reminded herself.

She glanced at him now, realised her hands were clenched in her lap and quickly relaxed them. He was studying her and now he frowned, and she couldn't help it, a small shiver of apprehension ran through her at the cold darkness in his eyes, the formidable set to his lips.

'Or perhaps there is a better question. Do *you* want to marry anyone else? It seems clear from your reaction that you do not want to marry me.'

The question was so unexpected it jolted her out of fear and an image crossed her mind, the floating wisps of a dream.

'I...'

'Elora—' his voice harsh '—I need the truth. Is there someone else?'

She managed to shake her head, but the hardness remained in his eyes, his gaze unwavering, as though he wanted to probe her mind. But she could see shadows there too, shadows that spoke of suspicion and anger. She knew that she would have to explain something, however much she didn't want to.

'There isn't anyone else.'

After all, where would she have found the opportunity to meet someone, given her sheltered upbringing? The closest to romance she'd ever got was a few hasty kisses with a visiting minor royal, mostly motivated by an extra glass of wine and a burning desire to at least experience a kiss, to come a little closer to her imaginings. And the experience hadn't been unpleasant, but neither had it lived up to her hopes and dreams. Not that her hopes and dreams had any basis in reality, but they were precious to her, and now she knew she had no choice but to expose them.

She could see disbelief grow in his eyes. 'It is hard to believe that, given your expression.'

How could this have happened? What was it about this man that unsettled her so much that she had lost her ability to dissemble, to hide all feelings behind a cool mask?

'It is still the truth,' she said firmly. 'There is no one else. It is simply…with this marriage, I have to put aside any dream I had of some*thing* different, however much I knew the dream to be impossible.'

To her surprise, she saw understanding in his eyes as they softened slightly.

'What was the dream?' he asked.

'It doesn't really matter—it's foolish. Just an idea. About a life where I can be less of a princess, less of a public figure.' Allowed to slip into anonymity, where she could find a job that didn't require her to have any sort of public persona whatsoever.

'A life where you can marry someone else?'

His voice was way gentler now, but his eyes were still hooded, dark, calculating and Elora knew she had to dissemble, that this was rocky ground, an emotional minefield she didn't understand.

'That wasn't something I had considered—I'd got as far as imagining living in a small house or an apartment, not a palace, of popping to the grocery store, maybe growing my own vegetables in an allotment.' There was no need to tell this dark, brooding prince about the shadowy mythical figure on the periphery of her dream. A gentle man, someone average, who maybe wore glasses, had a slightly receding hairline, someone with a kind smile. Someone who didn't know Princess Elora, someone who knew just Elora.

'It was an alternate reality, not one that could ever come to fruition.'

'Unless, of course, Caruli became a republic.'

Elora shook her head. 'And that is not something I can ever wish for.' How could she betray her very heritage, voice any desire to remove the crown from her parents' heads, to deprive her nephew of his birthright? 'So truly I know that was nothing but a foolish dream.'

Yet she could still see some doubt in his eyes and, without even thinking, she leant forward, reached out and touched his hand. 'Truly,' she repeated, the word ending on a slight gasp.

What had just happened? The feel of his hand under her fingers, the firm strength of his flesh sparked something she didn't recognise, an unfamiliar wave of heat, a clench of her tummy muscles that caused her to snatch her hand back. She looked down at it, shock, surprise and that strange heat widening her eyes, then glanced up at him, saw something in his eyes, a flash of an unfamiliar response she couldn't identify. Though whatever it was sent a shiver rippling over her skin.

Using all her willpower, she pushed the feelings down. Just as she knew how to hold anxiety at bay, so she would this, whatever this was. She forced her expression to become neutral, to wear the cool, impassive princess mask.

'That's the truth,' she said. 'There is no one else I want to marry.' She held his gaze, kept her voice level.

'OK,' he said, and he too now had himself in hand, no scowl, no emotion, and then for a moment his face lost some of its hardness. Perhaps there was even a hint of compassion in his dark eyes. 'I'm sorry, Elora, sorry that the dream of normality isn't possible. Whether you marry me or not.'

Her eyes narrowed. She didn't want pity. This was her choice as much as his and his hardship as much as hers. This was her future and, dammit, she was going to at least try to make the best of it.

Somehow.

Bracing herself, she forced a smile to her lips, a smile that could pass muster as genuine, tried and practised for use at all social occasions.

'So I guess we are going to do this?' she said, keeping her voice light and steady.

'I guess we are.'

'Was *that* a proposal?' she asked.

There was a pause and then he smiled, a small smile admittedly, but at least his lips upturned. And there it was again—she found herself looking at his mouth, studying that upturn, and a funny, unfamiliar sensation twisted in her tummy.

'I suppose it was.' Then the smile vanished.

'I am sure you pictured something more romantic than this. But I can see no point in dishonesty or hypocrisy. So I will not be going down on one knee with violins in the background.'

Elora heard the bitterness in his voice, wondered if he had done that for his first wife. All she remembered was the announcement of the engagement—that had been done with plenty of pomp and ceremony.

But what she, and probably everyone, remembered most was not the beginning of the marriage but the end—the stories that had swirled and grown. Stories of a beautiful wife, a celebrated actress with an adoring fanbase, already a European cinema idol, driven desperate with misery at the reception she'd received from the royal family. A woman who'd wished to continue with her career, the idea apparently frowned upon. Stories of how she had thrown herself on her husband's mercy, begging for help and release from the marriage. Stories of an escape plan, of night-time car chases and private helicopters. Speculation had been rife and, through it all, Elora's sympathies had been with Princess Caro, and she had hoped once a divorce went through that the Princess would find peace. Had been pleased when, a year later, there was news that she had remarried.

But there would be no escape route for Elora. No romance and no escape. But no matter.

She inclined her head now. 'There is no need to apologise. There are more important things to think about here than romance.'

'Yes, there are. If you are sure you wish to go ahead with it, we need to discuss how this marriage will work.'

This marriage—he didn't even use the word 'our'—and that was…wrong.

He'd clocked her reaction. 'What's wrong?' Yet the words themselves were said neutrally, almost with a dash of impatience.

'Nothing is wrong. But this marriage…it's not an abstract. It's our marriage.'

He shook his head. 'It is, but it isn't personal.'

No way could she let that go. 'Actually, yes, it is. Personal.' She needed to say this, now. He'd said he wanted honesty. Well, that went two ways, and this might be her only chance to have a proper conversation with him before chaperones and occasions took over. 'We're people.'

'No, Elora. That's the point. You are a princess. I am a prince. We are marrying as representatives of our countries. Sarala is wedding Caruli.'

'Yes.' She took a deep breath. 'But it's still personal. Part of this marriage is about the need for an heir.' Gritting her teeth, she found courage from somewhere, knew her cheeks were tinged with pink even as she spoke the words. 'Or perhaps it's better to say Sarala needs an heir, which means Sarala is also bedding Caruli. And that is personal. Up close and personal.'

Especially given at some future point she was going to have to explain, or she supposed he would figure it out, that she had never been bedded before.

If her mother had heard these words she would be horrified; perhaps Rohan was. But he didn't seem horrified. Instead, he was looking at her... differently. There was no coldness in his eyes now; they held an intentness, a focus, as if he were seeing her properly for the first time. Considering 'up close and personal'. Seeing her as a person and, for some reason, instead of filling her with disquiet, it was sending a little ripple of sensation over her skin. She caught her breath on a sudden gasp, but met his gaze full-on, tried to read what she saw there.

Then it was gone and he raised his hands.

'You're right. I'm sorry. That is a fair point. I want you to know that we can take our time with that side of things. We won't do anything until you're ready. Until we're both ready.'

'OK. Thank you.' Only as she looked at him now she was aware of just the faintest shiver of…disappointment? Ridiculous—what did she want? Rohan to carry her over his shoulder caveman-style to the bedroom? The image threatened to take hold in her mind and she pushed it away. Dear Lord. What was wrong with her?

She focused on what he was saying next.

'So, on a practical note, we should announce the engagement as soon as possible. I have no doubt our parents have got it all planned out. A pageant, a show, the sooner the people know the better.'

Elora frowned. She opened her mouth to speak and then closed it again. After all, it sounded as though the decision had been made.

'Don't you agree?'

'I… I'm not sure…'

But, before she could continue, the door swung open and an equerry came in. 'Announcing Their Majesties King Gaurav and Queen Joanna.'

Her parents.

CHAPTER THREE

ROHAN ROSE TO his feet, but not before he'd seen the change in Elora. Her face just seconds before had shown animation, a desire to share an opinion despite her clear anxiety about doing so. Now it was as though it had closed down, her expression remote, distant, an ice princess.

Thus she had looked when he'd entered the room, until… Until their gazes had locked and then there had been a flash, something in her clear, cool grey eyes, light as a single raincloud on a summer day.

He gave his head a small shake; the imagery was ridiculously poetic.

But something was going on. Because the remote ice princess façade had changed in the past half an hour. Perhaps encouraged by the knowledge that this was her chance to be honest, she had been surprisingly direct. Which was useful, because at least he knew what he needed to know. No one was forcing this bride into marriage.

Not that his first wife had been forced. Though that was what Caro had claimed at the end, in desperate self-defence of her betrayal. She'd said that he had coerced her, bullied her. At first he'd been stunned that anyone would believe that to be possible; Caro had been a famous actress when he'd met her, a friend of his older sister, a woman with a string of celebrity relationships behind her. Yet she had played the role of persecuted heroine so well, the press, the public... everyone had believed her.

But Elora was doing her duty of her own free will. As was he. As had their ancestors all those generations ago. Though she, like him, had expressed the wish for a normal life. The knowledge that she felt as he did had forged a strange tenuous connection, even if it was one there would be no point in discussing.

He stepped forward to kneel before his prospective in-laws for the traditional blessing and then rose to his feet, shot one more look at Elora, saw her glance at a portrait on the far wall before turning to bow her head in respect towards her parents.

King Gaurav stepped towards Rohan without even a glance at his daughter. 'Rohan. We thought it was time to join the meeting. There are details to sort out that need our presence.' The King's voice was assured, a man in no doubt of his authority. Like Rohan's father, he carried an aura, a sense of power and a sense that that power was deserved. A blood right.

Rohan knew that he lacked that surety, could not put his hand on his heart and say he deserved the power that came to him simply because he had been born the son of a king. It was a different matter at the negotiation table or in a boardroom full of business people. A different matter when he was acting on behalf of his country to promote it. There, Rohan knew his worth. Knew he was good at his job.

But here, standing by the ancient sword, surrounded by reminders of rulers gone by, it was possible to feel awed by the majesty of royalty, sense the aura of this King of Caruli.

Queen Joanna stepped forward and Rohan studied her. Saw the resemblance to Elora—the blonde hair, though now courtesy of an expensive hairdresser and toned to an ash-blonde, the grey eyes the same colour, but Queen Joanna's held hardness and calculation. She was still a beautiful woman, but her lips held a line of ingrained disapproval as she regarded him.

She spoke now. 'We will announce the engagement tomorrow—I assume you have brought appropriate clothing and necessities to remain here a few days. If not, we will, of course, be happy to send for them.'

Rohan frowned; he'd expected haste but not to this extent, especially not on this island. After all, he knew that Elora's older sister had given birth to a son. Prince Viraj was five and Caruli had an heir, had its succession in place.

On the other hand, this was what his parents had advocated—for Sarala, speed was essential. After all, he was not exactly beloved of the people of Sarala; it was better now than in the aftermath of his divorce, but he still had much to prove.

In which case, perhaps there was little point in delay; hadn't he himself said that to Elora only minutes before? Baluka had declared its republic status—time for royalty to strike back.

He sensed the smallest of movements next to him and turned to look at Elora, but her expression remained calm, serene and accepting.

Yet, minutes before, Elora had also had something to say, an opinion she'd wanted to voice. Why had her parents made a point of cutting their tête-à-tête short? Why the insistence on an announcement tomorrow? Why was the King acting as though his daughter wasn't even present in the room, as if she had no say? Rohan believed Elora had told him the truth, that she wasn't being forced to the altar. But what if he was wrong?

There was no doubt that she was different in

her parents' presence. In addition, there were further things he'd intended to discuss with his prospective bride, rules he'd wanted to set in place for the structure of their marriage. True, these things could be deferred until after the announcement but...

All his negotiating instincts were telling him he was being corralled. *They* were being corralled.

'Actually,' he said, and then stopped at the look of surprise on the King's face. 'Actually,' he repeated, 'I believe such an announcement is a little premature.' He raised a hand. 'Your daughter and I have agreed in principle to marriage. However, there is still much I would like to discuss with the Princess, prior to an official announcement. In fact, I was just about to ask her if she would do me the honour of having dinner with me tonight.'

There was silence, which Rohan made no move to break. He'd stated his position.

'Dinner.' The Queen uttered the word as though she'd never heard of the idea before. 'The two of you.'

'Yes. I would be delighted if the Princess came to Sarala and the palace there. Alternatively—' and now Rohan couldn't help himself '—if you give me access to the palace kitchens I would be happy to prepare a meal.' With luck, the suggestion would distract the Queen sufficiently from the idea of giving permission.

'Or perhaps, Mama—' Elora spoke for the first time since her parents' arrival '—I could cook for Rohan.'

'Then tomorrow, of course, we can meet to discuss the timing of an engagement. Like you, my parents are eager for an early announcement,' Rohan offered.

There was silence and now, finally, the King's gaze flickered to his daughter and then straight back to Rohan.

'Very well,' the King said. 'But tomorrow we need to finalise details. The people need to see this alliance.'

Elora bowed her head and the Queen stepped forward. 'Come, Elora.' She turned to Rohan. 'Dinner will be at seven-thirty. I will send a staff member to accompany you to the dining room. In the meantime, I hope you find the suite to your liking.'

A clear dismissal and equally clear injunction to remain in said suite until dinner, and Rohan accepted that. He had work to do after all. Work. Again, a bleakness settled over him. Would his work now have to come to an end? The business he had put so much into—would he have to sell up, liquidate? The thought filled him with a frustration that twisted his gut even as he knew he had to face the impending destiny he'd never wanted.

At precisely seven-thirty there was a knock on his door and Rohan went to open it, and smiled a welcome to the young man outside. He was slightly surprised when the palace staff member merely bowed the smallest of bows. 'Your Highness, I have been sent to escort you to dinner.' Somehow, the words managed to convey the utmost disapproval of both Rohan and the enterprise whilst still maintaining a rigid civility.

Perhaps, unlikely though it seemed, he was a budding republican. Whatever the reason, Pamir, who disclosed his name with palpable reluctance, maintained his distance for the whole journey down the magnificent staircase and along the palace corridors, past the imposing line of paintings and the gilded wooden panels.

He knocked at a door and this time Rohan decided to let him do his job and announce him, which he did with suitable words but a definite lack of fervour. Yet when he bowed to Elora his face creased into a genuine smile and Rohan blinked, waited until Pamir had left and turned to Elora. And blinked again, but for a different reason. Because there was no mistaking it this time—the gut punch of sudden, unexpected desire.

Dressed now in a more casual traditional *salwar kameez*, the calf-length, high-necked tunic a teal blue colour, with a floral pattern to reflect the teal, pink and white colours of the Carulian flag, over teal loose-fitting trousers, Elora looked beautiful, but it was more than that... Mere beauty wouldn't spark this sudden visceral reaction. Her glossy pure blonde hair was still pulled up but the style was slightly softer, allowing a few tendrils to escape, to frame the classic oval-shaped face. Her grey eyes seemed almost luminous and widened as she met his gaze. Now his eyes dropped to the curve of her lips, noted the generous shape, and the urge to step forward and pull her into his arms nigh on overwhelmed him.

Though of course he did nothing of the sort. Feet planted firmly on the ground, he tried to regroup, to find his usual poise, to regain control of this dinner and its agenda. This would be a marriage of convenience and he knew all too well from bitter experience how important it was to set rules in place before the event.

He nodded towards the door from which Pamir had departed. 'You have a definite fan there.'

'I have known Pamir all my life. The three of us played in...' She broke off and he knew she must be speaking of her brother, Prince Sanjay, whose life had tragically ended in an accident aged eleven.

'I'm sorry—' he began.

'Thank you.' Her voice was colourless but definite, the spark that had been there just seconds before extinguished. 'But there is no need to say any more.' She clearly had no intention of expanding on the subject and he didn't blame her. Yet he'd seen the flash of raw grief in her eyes, knew the memory had triggered a pain he couldn't fathom. Elora and Sanjay had been twins and he couldn't imagine what his loss must have meant to her. He wanted to offer comfort, but he sensed it wouldn't be welcomed. Especially not from him.

'Please be seated, Your Highness,' she continued, her voice both formal and aloof. 'The food is in chafing dishes to keep warm. I will serve you when you are ready.'

'No.' The refusal was instinctive. 'I am happy to serve myself.'

'As you wish.' She bowed her head and his eyes narrowed as he wondered if her parents had spent the day instructing her on how to behave at dinner. To present herself as a dutiful wife-to-be, allay any doubts that Rohan might have.

'That *is* what I wish. I also wish to apologise. When I asked you to dinner I didn't intend for you to have to cook it yourself.'

'It was no trouble.'

'Is that the truth?' He asked the question abruptly in the hope it might provoke an honest answer.

'Yes.' And this time her voice sounded more definite. 'I enjoy cooking.'

He studied her expression. 'For real? Or do you think that is the "right" answer? I would like us to continue to be honest with each other.'

He gesticulated with one hand as he spoke to emphasise his point, just as she did the same as she opened her mouth to speak, and, before he could pull back, their hands collided. It was the merest of accidental brushes and yet the effect caused him to hold his breath. It had sparked a current, a shimmer in the air that made them both look down at their hands as if in wonder.

She recovered herself first, fast enough that he wondered if he'd imagined the whole thing, though he knew he hadn't. On his part, anyhow.

But better to ignore it. Until he'd figured out what to do about it. On the one hand, of course it was positive if he and Elora were attracted to each other, but…he had no wish for an attraction that felt so…intense. An attraction that had the potential to distract him from what would be way more important in this marriage. Structure, rules, control.

'It is the truth.' Her voice was slightly breathless and this time she kept talking, he guessed as a distraction from whatever had just happened. 'Honestly, I've always liked to cook. When I was a child I spent as much time as I could in the palace kitchens and one of the sous chefs befriended me. Pamir's mother, in fact. She showed me how to bake and I loved it. Then...' she paused a fraction of a beat '...later, as I grew older, the kitchen became a place where I could be me. When I cook, I stop being a princess. If that makes sense.'

'It does,' he said. That was how he felt when he was involved in his business, where he was simply Rohan Carmody, a name he'd derived from his royal dynastic name, Kamodian.

'It's a chance to create something in different ways. You can follow a recipe or adapt it or have a go at making things up from scratch. Can suit your creation to your mood.' He knew that her love of cooking was genuine; there was real enthusiasm on her face and the animation gave her vitality and assurance. 'When I'm cooking I can kind of zone out from real life.' She stopped and bit her lip as if in annoyance at giving away too much. 'Anyway, as I said, it was no trouble to cook tonight.'

'Now I do believe you and I am looking forward to eating what you've cooked.' He hesitated. 'But is it OK if we talk first? So I'm not distracted by the food.' It was going to be hard enough not to be distracted by the tug of awareness that was refusing to disappear, even in the flow of conversation.

'Of course. Please go ahead.'

'Shall we sit?'

She nodded and they sat at the perfectly set dining table, a centrepiece of flowers exuding both colour and a light pleasant scent. Linen napkins and silver cutlery gleamed and there were candles in the elaborate silver candlesticks.

'So what room is this?' he asked.

'This is known as the meeting chamber. The history books say it is where important lords would be invited to private conversations—near the kitchen so that one trusted servant could bring food and drink easily and safely. It is used for similar purposes nowadays. I like it because I used to sit in here and read recipe books.'

For a moment he could picture a younger Elora sitting with legs curled under her, hiding from the realities of the palace and escaping into a world of ingredients.

'This feels like a good place then. I felt we were interrupted this morning before we'd had a chance to finish our discussion of what happens next. When I suggested we announce the engagement soon I got the feeling you disagreed.

When your parents suggested it, though, you said nothing.'

'Nothing I say would change my parents' minds.' The words were a simple statement of fact, not bitter.

'OK. But *I* will listen. And if we are in agreement together, we will be able to change their minds. I will listen,' he repeated, sensing her reluctance and seeing the doubt in her eyes. But not just doubt, surprise as well at his words. Clearly, Elora wasn't used to being listened to. That or she hadn't thought he was the sort of man who paid attention. He waited, let the silence speak for itself, then risked a smile. 'But I need something to listen to.'

Then she gave a small smile of her own and he felt as though there had been some level of acceptance.

'Fair point,' she said. One more second to marshal her thoughts and then, 'I understand why this marriage is a good idea. For our countries.' If not for them. The words were unspoken but no less poignant for that. 'But the idea is to reassure the people that the monarchies of Caruli and Sarala are stable and present and will continue. That the rule of their kings will go on fairly and justly, so there is no need for a republic.'

'Agreed.'

'But I believe it is about more than that. Reassurance that something will continue is not enough to make people not want change.' She paused, seeming to replay the sentence in her head. 'Even people who support the monarchy may not want it to continue as it always has.'

Rohan stared at her, struck by the observation and its truth. He himself felt like that, so did Marisa, and there was every chance that Elora's older sister Flavia did too. So if they, as the younger generation of royals, felt like that, so too would the people.

'They want to see that we've moved with the times, that some things have changed since our ancestors' days.'

Elora nodded and for the first time that day she smiled a real smile that lit her grey eyes and revealed an unexpected dimple in her left cheek and a sudden breathlessness threatened him.

'Exactly. And seeing us rush into marriage won't show that at all. Two people who don't know each other. Some people will decry it as a political move that insults their intelligence, others will dislike the idea that two young people are marrying simply for political reasons, others will feel that we are being forced into it and that that is wrong.' She hesitated. 'I know that is what Pamir feels; that is why he was so reticent with you. He is fond of me and he suspects what is going on and he believes it is wrong for me to be rushed into marriage, especially…'

She broke off abruptly and Rohan had little doubt about what words she'd cut off and a sudden surge of anger ran through him.

'You may as well say it, Elora. Finish the sentence. He doesn't want you to be rushed into marriage, especially with me, given my reputation as a terrible husband.' Terrible didn't really cover it, but he'd rather be thought of as a cruel, unfeeling bastard than for the truth to be known. And it seemed clear that Elora believed every one of those rumours and speculations, believed in the portrait the press had painted, and for an instant that fed the anger, turned it into an ice-cold hurt, even though he knew he could hardly blame her. 'I get it. The press may take this and come up with a sacrificial lamb story, which isn't what we want at all.'

'I don't think we can ignore that the people, especially those on Caruli, may feel that. I am their princess.'

And much as he loathed having to ask the next question, he knew he must. 'What about how you feel? Do you see yourself as a sacrificial lamb?'

'No.' But the denial held a thread of doubt and now the anger and hurt morphed into sudden compassion. How was Elora supposed to know the truth? If she believed even one half of the speculation she was probably terrified of him.

'Elora, look at me. Please.' She raised her head and did so. 'I don't want to discuss my previous marriage—it is water under the bridge and in the past.' A past he would not revisit. 'But I promise I will do my best to be a good husband. You have no need to be afraid of me.' He could only hope the words rang true, even as he knew they were words he would say even if they weren't truth.

Her grey eyes looked into his, unreadable pools of shimmering silver, and she gave a small tentative nod. An acknowledgement, he hoped, that she had at least registered the words, so perhaps something had been achieved, a small measure of trust, however fragile.

'So now I'd like to hear how you think we should present this marriage to the people.'

'As a positive thing, so we need a positive spin.'

'What sort of spin?' He knew he wasn't going to like this.

'A romance.'

Rohan stared at her, every instinct crying out against something so patently ridiculous. 'You want us to spin a romance, pretend we're in love, act all lovey-dovey.' He couldn't help the horror in his voice. 'It won't work. No one would believe it.'

'Why not?'

'Because I am not a romantic type of guy.'

'I get that.' Her voice was cool, nonjudgmental, and against his will he felt sympathy for her. He wondered if she had ever dreamt of romance, but reminded himself that she must have known a political marriage was most likely for her. 'You don't have to *be* romantic, you just have to pretend. This would be the story. Now Baluka has become a republic, it is natural for you to be recalled. It is also natural for our families to confer, to work together and to want to show the people that we are good rulers with a plan. Agreed?'

'So far,' Rohan said cautiously.

'So, as Sarala's ambassador, you have come to Caruli today to meet my parents and discuss ways for Sarala and Caruli to work together. Whilst you're here you also meet me and we…' Now she blushed. 'We like each other and you ask me to dinner.'

As he looked at her, somehow, that whole fiction didn't seem so impossible. Because, dammit, something was going on here. If he'd met Elora back in London, if she hadn't been a princess, and there'd been this zing of desire, maybe he would have asked her to dinner. Or maybe he wouldn't, because he wouldn't have trusted the intensity of the desire. He knew desire didn't last, still recalled the wild, heady days of his marriage to his first wife. After Caro, he'd taken a different approach to relationships—attraction, sure, but nothing that wasn't under control. Nothing that made him care.

Undaunted by his silence, she continued, though her voice faltered slightly. 'Then we go from there. We plan various dates; we can use them to get out and about. I can show you Caruli, you can show me Sarala. It will be great publicity, and give us a chance to give our views, travel around, and show the people who we are, who the next generation is.'

Rohan studied her, saw the intensity in her grey eyes. Her arguments were lucid and made sense and he was struck anew by the difference in her here and now, compared to the princess he'd met earlier in the day. Was aware again of that simmer of desire, knew too that desire was only an added complication. Right now, this marriage had to be all about measured decisions, about avoiding another disaster like his previous marriage.

'Those are all valid arguments,' he acknowledged. He knew too what she wasn't saying, that her way would show the world that this would be a different marriage to the one that went before, that she was no sacrificial lamb, that she was

going into this marriage of her own free will.
Proof would be in the spinning of a romance.

'So do you want to go ahead?'

Did he?

Aware of her steady gaze, he considered the
strategy.

CHAPTER FOUR

THERE WAS A long silence and although Rohan's expression was impassive Elora sensed he was considering the idea, assessing the pros and cons and its viability. A look of weariness crossed his face, weariness mixed with distaste, and she felt a pang of hurt—a hurt that years of practice enabled her to instantly mask. A quick glance down at her folded hands was enough to allow her to put the expression of serene acceptance back onto her face. At least he had considered the idea, not dismissed it out of hand.

Yet when she looked back up she saw that his dark eyes were watching her.

'It is a good idea…'

'But?' she asked. 'But it is too much effort and will be too difficult for you to pretend to be attracted to me. I understand.'

Elora was sure she had kept any note of bitterness from her voice—after all, she did understand. But what she hadn't expected was the crack of laughter that greeted her words and she couldn't keep the surprise from her face.

'What's so funny?'

Rohan shook his head. 'That's not what I was thinking. At all. I mean you're right—it will be an effort, but not because I can't pretend to be attracted to you. That won't be a problem.'

Elora bit her lip, held back the urge to ask what he meant. Did he mean he was attracted to her? The idea sent an unfamiliar shiver down her spine, clenched her tummy muscles, caused her eyes to linger suddenly on his lips, his hands, the sheer strength he exuded.

Get a grip. He'd said it would be easy to pretend—all that meant was that he knew how to act, play to the camera. But… The way he was looking at her, right here and now… There was heat in his dark eyes. She was sure of it. Nearly sure.

Though how was she to tell, to know? She had no idea how to play this game, no inkling of the rules. All she did know was that she had no intention of making a fool of herself.

Keeping her voice cool, she said, 'I'm glad to hear you are confident in your acting skills. You'll have to give me some tips. If we go ahead with this. So what were you going to say?'

She kept her gaze neutral, her chin at a slightly defiant tilt, and waited.

'I was going to say that I am not sure you are truly aware of what you are taking on. Not just with me but with the press. Your idea means we will be on show, playing the part of two people falling in love, and we'll need to be convincing because, trust me, the press will want its pound of flesh and they'll be scrutinising every move, every word, every look, and it won't always be under our control. They will rake things up and speculate, and that can be difficult. I can't let you go into this without really considering what you will be putting yourself through. And the consequences if we can't pull it off.'

She saw the shadows cloud his eyes and knew he spoke from bitter experience, remembered exactly how the press had torn into him, their persistence, the stories and opinions and… For a second, sympathy threatened. Until she recalled the facts—or at least what had surely been the facts. Princess Caro had accused her husband of cold-hearted cruelty. And Rohan had never once, personally or through a spokesman, so much as issued a denial, had made no comment whatso-ever, made no attempt to put his side of the story, never refuted a single one of the claims.

Never given his side, presumably because there was no side to give.

But now, as she looked at him, Elora was aware of a sliver of doubt as to his guilt. Cold maybe, but cruel? He'd shown no sign of cruelty, but then again, he'd said himself he was a good actor—maybe all of this, the dinner, the meeting was an act. Judging by the grim set of his mouth now, she had little doubt that he could be ruthless

'I understand that the press will be intrusive and ever-present, but there is not a lot they can do to hurt me. My past is an open book.' She took a deep breath. 'But I understand this will be difficult for you, so really it is your call. If the inevitable coverage of your first marriage will be too…' What word to use? Her brain spun as she saw the set of his lips, the darkness in his eyes '…painful I understand that.'

The wrong adjective, though she suspected any word she'd picked would have been wrong as the grim expression hardened.

She hurried on. 'But maybe you could come up with a way you want us to combat it.'

'We will not speak about my first marriage. Not to the press, not to anyone.'

Elora bowed her head, pushed down the sudden surge of anxiety that threatened. Because when Rohan looked like that, so formidable, so withdrawn, the doubts could only multiply. What was she getting herself into?

'Understood,' she said. 'The decision is yours. I would like to try the fake romance angle, but again it is up to you.'

There was a second of hesitation and then he nodded, held out a hand. 'Then we have a deal.'

Elora hesitated. Doubt shot into her head—what if her mother was wrong and Elora did have fertility issues? No. She would not think that, would not let an anxiety, a weakness affect this decision, use it as an excuse to allow her not to marry this man, do her duty. Earn redemption. Her mother was right; she had done enough damage already. The memory of her words jolted pain through her and also a dose of determination. She would do this for Caruli, and maybe her mother would show her some respect, some semblance of affection. Perhaps her father would feel something positive about her.

Abruptly, she put her hand out, watched as if in slow motion he took it in his, and then she wasn't sure what happened. It felt as though a current shot up her arm at his touch, as if she could see sparks fly, and her reaction was so extreme, so out of her comfort zone she couldn't cover it. She dropped his hand and stared at him, wide-eyed.

'I… Food…' she gabbled. 'Now we've made that decision, let's have food.' The idea calmed her as she thought about the meal she'd prepared, ran through the components, the menu, and she managed to rise with her usual poise at least mostly intact.

Rohan nodded, though she was sure he rose with unseemly haste, after a quick glance down at his own hand. But by the time they returned to their seats with their loaded plates he seemed unflustered, sat down and waited for her before tasting his own food. She saw the surprise in his eyes as he chewed and swallowed and then looked up at her.

'This is amazing.'

Now she smiled, a real smile, because she knew he wasn't faking this. 'Thank you. I'm glad you like it. It is a Carulian speciality with a royal history, so it seemed appropriate.'

'Tell me.'

'So, years ago, Carulian kings were avid hunters—as you know, Caruli is known for its wild horses and royalty liked nothing better than to go out hunting. But they also liked to eat the meat as fresh as possible, so they would take their royal chefs with them on the hunt. Royalty also wanted their meat to be properly cooked and to smell good. Not always easy for a chef presented with a freshly killed boar or deer. So this dish was born—basically, those chefs figured out they needed to carry a whole host of ingredients with them and as time went on they perfected the recipe. Apparently, King Aadarsh about a hundred years ago chased the royal chef around the eating area because the dish was too bland.'

'Well, I promise I won't be chasing you round the table because of that.'

There was a momentary silence and Elora bit back a mad urge to ask if there were any other reasons why he would chase her round the table, and pushed away the idea that she probably wouldn't run very fast.

'You wouldn't need to,' she said without thinking, replayed the words in her head and hurried on. 'I mean, one of the ingredients in this is hot chilli peppers, along with cumin, coriander, melon seeds, peppercorns, ginger. Oh, and it isn't made with wild boar any more either—I've used chicken, and I've added my own twist. Lime and a bit of paprika.'

'Well, the whole thing is incredible.'

'And these look good too.' He pointed as he spoke.

'I cooked the bread in the tandoor oven, the rice is just plain but I've made it as fluffy as possible and there is a simple *raita* to go with it. I thought that would cool it down. I don't know how hot or spicy you like things.' She looked at him. 'Your food, I mean. Obviously.' *For heaven's sake.*

For a moment she thought she saw a gleam of amusement in his eyes.

'So, do you cook a lot? For family?'

Elora shook her head. 'My parents don't really understand or approve of my cooking. They believe there are more important things to do.'

'Do you agree?'

'Of course. I understand that part of being a princess is a lifestyle that involves having a palace chef and kitchen staff. But I do love cooking and it can be a useful skill. That's why I decided to…' Elora broke off, aware that she was so unused to anyone showing an interest in her that she'd nearly said something she had no intention of sharing.

'Why you decided to do what?'

'Nothing. It doesn't matter.'

'Then why can't you tell me?' The question was eminently reasonable.

'Because it's not something I've told anyone, so I'd rather keep it to myself.'

'OK, but, for the record, you can trust me. We've just made a deal to fake a relationship, to get married.'

'As a deal,' Elora said softly. 'We still don't really know each other. Trust has to be earned.' And she didn't know if she could ever trust a man who'd treated his ex-wife as he apparently had. A man who had made it clear that marriage was off-limits as a topic to his soon-to-be second wife. 'Would you tell me something, share a secret with me?'

'It would depend on the secret.'

'There you are. This is a secret I propose to keep.'

'Fair enough, and I agree that trust has to be earned. But there are some things that we will have to trust each other on going forward.'

'Such as?' She heard a heaviness in his voice, and suddenly the enormity of what they were planning struck her anew. She took another forkful of food and focused on identifying the flavours. The slight bitterness of the cumin, the tart lime, the sweetness of the smoked paprika and the bite of chilli all grounded her.

'I need to trust that you will behave appropriately; you cannot cause any scandal. Your reputation must be spotless. Not only now but throughout our married life. No scandal, no negative publicity. And that means fidelity. If you have any doubts about that, then this will not work. The press will sniff out any indiscretion and I will not tolerate seeing my wife splashed across the papers with another man.'

A sudden anger lacerated her at his tone and at his words and Elora narrowed her eyes. 'I understand you don't know me, Rohan, but I wouldn't do that to you or anyone. There will be no indiscretions. And,' she couldn't help adding, 'I am not the one with the track record of being splashed across the papers with a partner. So can I check where you stand on the fidelity front? One rule for you, one for me?'

After all, she knew that was the way of the world. Her sister's husband had been rumoured to have had an affair, but the expectation had been that Flavia would forgive and forget. She had a suspicion that her own father had strayed even as her mother had turned a blind eye, too worried that her husband would divorce her for failing to produce another heir.

Anger flared in his eyes for a moment, but no way would she back down.

Then, unexpectedly, Rohan's expression relaxed, his lips even turned up in the smallest of smiles. 'Fair point and fair question. In answer, I play fair. I will not expose my wife to the humiliation of seeing me splashed across the papers with another woman. You can trust me on that. Can I trust you?'

'Yes.'

But as they looked at each other she knew that, once again, these were only words. Trust did have to be earned over time. But maybe for now they needed to believe that it was a possibility. But how to make that start? She had to try.

Perhaps he felt the same, as he leaned over

and gently covered her hand with his own. 'Then that's a good start.'

The words accentuated the sense of warmth, of promise that his touch was generating, causing a swirl of conflicting feelings. A heat, a desire that caused her to tentatively reach out and cover his hand in hers in acknowledgement.

She heard his own swiftly concealed intake of breath, which he tried to mask by clearing his throat, and her whole being was focused on their still clasped hands, dwelt on the sensation of his skin beneath hers.

'A good start,' she managed, and now she wasn't even sure what they were talking about any more. Her lips had parted and his dark gaze focused on her mouth and she was leaning forward, and so was he and she knew she needed to break the spell. She pulled her hands back and for a second she froze, their gazes enmeshed, and then she scrambled ungracefully to her feet.

'I... How about dessert?' She gave what she recognised herself as a slightly breathless laugh. 'Luckily, it's ice cream.' *Really*, Elora... Perhaps she should suggest they bathe in it? 'Well, not ice cream, more of a *kulfi*. But I even got cones.'

'Then I have an idea.' She wasn't sure if she was imagining it, but his voice held something, something that surely couldn't be shock. 'Why don't we go for a moonlit stroll? You can show me the palace gardens.' His voice gained assurance. 'It could be a part of our story. We have an evening stroll and eat ice cream.'

'Good idea.'

'And we could talk as well.'

'About what?'

'About next steps, a more detailed plan, and exactly what we need to do to pull this off.'

It was a good point. If they were going to pull this off in the face of intense press scrutiny, they would need to be convincing. Would have to act as though they liked each other—would have to act as though they were attracted to each other.

That could be crucial, the make-or-break pivot.

Problem was, right now, Elora didn't understand what was going on, had a horrible suspicion that she was actually really attracted to Rohan. It was an unforeseen development and she had no idea what to do about it. In which case, she would have to pretend to be pretending about an attraction she had no desire to feel.

And then her gaze lingered on his lips, fell to his hands, imagined them around her waist, tugging her body against his, pictured her lips parting, her own hands in his thick, dark hair, pulling him closer... Elora gulped, felt heat rush to her face and over her body. The flush of awareness signalled a sense of panic, and from somewhere she pulled a final vestige of poise and could only hope that Rohan hadn't clocked any of her ridiculously out of control reactions.

'Sure. Good plan,' was the best she could come up with as she forced herself to walk from the room with all the grace and poise she had spent so many years cultivating, and which this man was threatening to dismantle in mere hours.

CHAPTER FIVE

Rohan took a deep breath as he watched Elora leave the room and head for the kitchen, aware of the need to pull his thoughts together, pull *himself* together and stop being so poleaxed by a brush of their hands, so distracted by her lips.

Because they had to figure out how to make this fake romance plan work, however much the word *romance* set his teeth on edge. He recalled the futile, gauche, unwanted romantic gestures he'd made in an attempt to fathom his first marriage and he could almost taste the bitter aftertaste of humiliation. He'd been a fool, a credulous fool, and he'd paid the price.

But this was different; this was a planned romance.

An illusion.

One that made political sense.

He looked up as Elora returned, carefully holding two cones, each topped with a light green scoop. He rose and headed towards her, and there it was again, a hum, a zing, a visceral reaction triggered by…by Elora. He wasn't sure if it was the gloss of her hair, the grey of her eyes, the tilt of her chin or the tantalising scent of rose petals. Whatever it was, it kept catching him unawares, shocking him with its volatility.

He took his proffered cone, noted how careful they both were to avoid even an accidental touch.

'Thank you.'

'You're welcome. Follow me. I agree we should see the palace gardens. They are illuminated and a truly beautiful place to walk. I've grown up with them and they still fill me with awe. If we need to, it will be easy to describe a romantic stroll there.'

'Sounds ideal.' He tasted the *kulfi* and turned to her, genuinely distracted from his thoughts. 'This is also amazing.'

For a fleeting second she smiled, and then her eyes narrowed slightly. 'You don't have to say that.'

'I know that and I wouldn't lie. We're trying to build trust, remember? This is truly delicious. Another Elora twist?'

'Yup. I put pistachios and almonds in it, and a little bit of cocoa powder.'

'I'd forgotten how much I like *kulfi*. The past few years I've not had it so I've settled for ice cream, but this…' He looked down at the light green concoction and could see the flecks of nuts in it. 'I should probably know this, but what's the actual difference?'

'*Kulfi* doesn't include eggs and uses full fat milk so it's creamier. It's also denser because it's simmered overnight and it isn't whipped. It apparently originated in the sixteenth century. They used to mix the ingredients, put it into pots and bury them so they'd get cold.' She gave a sudden smile. 'Sorry, I like knowing the origins of food—it's just so incredible to think that people all those centuries ago ate a version of what we are eating right now.'

He walked along the trellised pathway, under the arches, lush with deep green foliage, inhaled the heady scent of the flowers and saw the riotous, gorgeous mix of colours that seemed to glow iridescent in the moonlight.

'Perhaps a prince and princess centuries ago walked along this path eating that version,' he said.

'That's a nicer image of the past than blood and gore and daggers and swords,' she said. 'These gardens were built by one of my ancestors, King Eshanth, for his wife, who was apparently one of the most beautiful women on the island. They married for love and these gardens were an ongoing work of art. They built three terraces and planted an amazing number of trees and a mix of flowers. And this.'

She came to a halt and so did he, stunned by the magical backdrop ahead of him. A waterfall cascaded over a stone parapet, the water a melodious gush, an illuminated flow that twinkled and glittered, lit by strategically placed lights in the niches behind it.

'It's magical,' he said.

'Straight out of a fairy tale,' she replied as she finished her last bit of *kulfi*. 'So we have a perfect setting for romance, but how are we going to make everyone believe the romance itself is real?'

They headed to a bench set close enough to the waterfall to be bewitched by its beauty and for the noise to be an accompaniment rather than an impediment to conversation. The bench itself nestled on a patio area vibrant with shrubs and bushes. And suddenly as he turned to her all he could think was that the setting, beautiful though it was, served only as a backdrop for her beauty. The moonlight glinted off her silvery blonde hair and highlighted the delicate strength of her features—the wide brow, her luminous grey eyes and lips that seemed to beg to be kissed.

He had to focus, had to keep talking...

'Well, a key point will be to convince them that we are attracted to each other.' He sounded like a pompous professor but that was better than succumbing to the urge to kiss her.

'How?' The question was blunt. 'You said ear-lier you weren't worried about pretending to be attracted to me. You've clearly already figured it out. So tell me.'

'Well, actually…' Rohan paused, suddenly wishing he still had the *kulfi*, something to dis-tract him. All his aplomb had disappeared and although the evening had a pleasant breeze he felt perspiration threaten, his collar seeming to tighten around his neck as she looked at him expectantly. 'That's not exactly what I meant.'

Her grey eyes were wide and, dammit, he couldn't tell what she was thinking.

'So what did you mean?' There was the slight-est frown on her forehead, her lips upturned in what could be an encouraging smile. And now he seemed incapable of tearing his gaze from her mouth. Forcing himself to look away, to focus on the rush and cascade of the waterfall, he tried to decide what to do. He'd been planning on telling her the truth, admitting the damned attraction, but standing here, looking at her wide-eyed in-nocence, he knew he couldn't. Or wouldn't.

Thoughts ran through his head at lightning speed. Unless the attraction was mutual, and he was by no means sure it was, the knowledge could spook her, couldn't help but make her feel awkward. Better if she believed for now that the attraction was as fake as the romance. Something to be worked on.

But it was more than that, he acknowledged to himself deep down. To tell Elora of this attraction would be to give her power over him. Even more so if it were one-sided. He'd believed Caro had been attracted to him, had thought his own feelings had been reciprocated, and he'd been made a fool of. Because he'd ceded control.

He wouldn't take that risk again. He didn't understand his awareness of Elora, the visceral tug of desire that he couldn't seem to control. Well, he would learn to control it, tame the volatility. Would also try to figure out how Elora felt about him. And then would be the time for complete transparency.

Right now, the most important thing was to convince the world that their relationship was a real one, and that meant keeping things under control. So he needed to think fast, because Elora was still looking at him expectantly.

'I meant that we are both used to being on public display and as such we are used to projecting feelings that aren't real, or hiding feelings that are. So, between us, we should be able to figure out how to make the press believe this is real.'

Elora's gaze was steady but he'd swear something flashed across her eyes. Hurt? Disappointment? Or perhaps it was simple relief.

'You're right in that I know how to project certain feelings, but faking attraction is new to me.'

'Me too, so I guess we'll need to practice.'

Even as he said the words, he realised how foolhardy they were.

'Practice how?' There was a definite hint of panic in her voice. 'Practice what? I mean, it's not as though I'm going to be plastering myself all over you on a first date.' There was silence and now she'd said the words the image filled his mind, of her doing exactly that, her body against his, her hair tickling his nose, the delicate tilt of her head as she looked up at him, lips parted.

Hell. Rohan focused on staying stock-still, and realised that he wasn't the only one with a dreamy look on their face. Elora was staring at him, her grey eyes wide and slightly out of focus, as if her mind might be headed down the same path as his.

Rohan gritted his teeth. All he wanted to do was lean forward and kiss her but…he wouldn't. Dammit, he would show himself that he could control this, because he would not let this marriage be governed by desire in any way at all, wouldn't let attraction make him lose sight of anything, let it con him into believing he cared or, worse, that he was cared for. This marriage was going to be played by the rulebook and he had every intention of making the rules.

Digging deep, Rohan found the prince capable of banter and charm, of lightness and flirtation. 'So, on which date do you think plastering is acceptable?' he asked, careful to inject a light tone to his voice, hopeful that this would deflate the sudden tension in the air, relieved when she tilted her chin and met his gaze full-on.

'There will be no plastering,' she said. 'That isn't how a Carulian princess would behave in public, however modern she is.'

'And in private?' The words fell from his lips without thought and her face became tinged with pink.

But she didn't miss a beat. 'Right now, this princess is only concerned with her public image. And,' she continued, and now her voice was matter-of-fact, in control, 'I don't think we need to worry too much—we won't be expected to do any lovey-dovey stuff on a first date after all.'

'No, but we need to at least look comfortable.'

She raised her eyebrows. 'Comfortable? That sounds like a pair of cosy old slippers. We're meant to be giving people something to be excited about.'

'I get that, but nervous isn't a good look either.'

'I am not nervous.'

In lieu of a reply, he stretched out a hand and she shifted backwards, nearly lost her balance, grabbed the table edge to steady herself and glared at him.

'You caught me by surprise.'

'Doesn't matter. We could get caught on camera in an unguarded moment. And there needs to be a spark.'

She looked at him, jutted her chin out. 'There will be. I've got this. I just need a little bit of time. To adapt. You were right, I do know how to project an image. By tomorrow there will be sparks galore. But first we need to run this past our parents.'

He thought for a minute. 'Let's get your parents on board first. Sarala needs this marriage slightly more than Caruli does. So if your parents agree, my parents should follow. Would you prefer to talk to them on your own?'

Elora looked at him as though he were mad. 'I don't think that's the way to go,' she said.

'Why not?'

'It doesn't matter. It would just be best if you present the idea. That's all.'

'I need more than that. If you want me to negotiate to convince them, I have to understand more about the dynamics. If there's anything I should or shouldn't say or do, I need to know now.'

He sensed her reluctance, but then she nodded understanding.

'Basically, it will be best if you do all the talking. Say it is your idea, your plan—if they believe that, they are more likely to go along with it. More likely to see the positives. Leave me out of it as much as you can. Play the overbearing prince card.' As she rose he'd swear he heard her mutter, 'Well, that should come easy.'

Elora felt her heart thud against her ribcage as they entered the Treasure Room. She glanced sideways at Rohan, aware of an illogical urge to take his hand. To offer comfort or give it? Neither made sense. Rohan looked completely confident, no sign of nerves, apart from perhaps a slight tautening of his jawline. As for comfort—why would she expect to get that from Rohan's touch? Or maybe she just craved that touch, which was mortifying, seeing as he had made it plain that any attraction would have to be faked. In any case, she had no intention of reaching out; to do so would do nothing but court her parents' disapproval. They would see that as unnecessary, an unbecoming display of emotion.

Enough. She stepped forward and bowed her head in greeting to her parents, but not before she caught the sharp glance her mother levelled at her. Her father, as always, ignored her, kept his gaze averted, focused on Rohan.

'Thank you for seeing us so late,' Rohan said. 'We thought it would be courteous and useful to tell you what we have decided.'

King Gaurav's eyebrows went up. 'I would be interested in hearing what you *discussed*.'

Rohan's smile was still assured. 'Of course we value Your Majesties' opinions,' he said smoothly.

'So tell us your thoughts,' the Queen said.

'I believe that the people would not welcome a rushed marriage, would not wish to see their Princess pushed into a political marriage with a man with a reputation like mine. I think it would therefore serve the purpose of both Sarala and Caruli if we offer them a romance. A fairy tale—this would give both the Princess and myself an opportunity to make a number of public appearances in a positive light and then announce our engagement when, hopefully, it can be welcomed by the people as a real alliance.'

The Queen's face darkened and Elora felt a sense of dread, though a quick glance at her father's face showed her that he was considering the facts. She knew that in public the Queen would never question the word of the King. Even in private she had become less assured since Sanjay's death, had lived in fear that the King would divorce her and remarry for an heir. Perhaps he would have if Flavia hadn't had a son, if there wasn't now an heir. But there was and her mother had regained some of her lost authority and influence. But not all.

The King nodded. 'Your words do make some level of sense. I have heard from my own sources and there is much in what you say—there is a feeling that we royals must modernise.' He sighed. 'I am now too old a dog to change, but your generation and the next perhaps should make a start.' For a fleeting instant his gaze rested on Elora and, as always, skittered away again. Grief tugged at her heart. Sanjay had been her father's pride and joy, the beacon for the future. Her mother resented her, but her father… Elora believed he simply wished her away, could not bear the sight of his daughter and the memories she evoked of all he'd lost.

'So you agree to the plan?' Rohan asked.

'I agree to the commencement of the plan, but we will need to monitor the results. If adverse publicity is generated or anything looks to be going wrong then the engagement will be announced immediately.'

Rohan nodded. 'I agree that we should evaluate how the idea is going in two weeks and discuss the best way forward from there.'

Elora held her breath, as aware as everyone else in the room that her father was used to being agreed with one hundred per cent without caveats, but the King gave the smallest of smiles.

'Very well, young man. Have it your way. For now. Provided, of course, your parents agree.'

'That shouldn't be an issue. So we can start tomorrow.' Rohan turned to Elora but before he could speak the Queen interceded.

'Elora looks tired and I would like the chance of a mother-daughter chat before we sleep. I am sure you wish to apprise your parents of events. I will finalise plans for tomorrow and you will be contacted as to arrangements.'

Elora focused on keeping her expression neutral even as she felt anxiety surge. Mother-daughter moments were rare but only happened when Elora had displeased her parents by more than the fact she simply existed. But she would weather the scolding, the lecture, the hectoring and if she could she would do as her mother wished. At least, whatever happened, her father had consented to the plan.

Next to her, she sensed Rohan's glance and looked up at him, aware of her mother's gaze.

'I will see you tomorrow, Your Highness,' she said.

'Until then,' he said. 'And thank you for today.' And he smiled at her, a real smile that held warmth and…a sense of promise… It was a smile that tingled her toes and surprised her.

Elora smiled back, watched as he left the room, aware of a sudden desire to run after him, and perhaps he sensed that because at the door he stopped and turned. But the Queen rose and headed to Elora, her lips thinned, her grey eyes cold and hard.

'Come,' she said and, reaching out, she turned her daughter away from the door as she raised a hand in dismissal.

Elora turned her head and she too raised a hand, knew it would be better to simply get the mother-daughter moment over with.

She followed her mother through the second door and up the spiral staircase to the room the Queen used for private meetings, turned to her mother and braced herself as she registered the anger on Queen Joanna's classically beautiful features.

'Fool,' her mother spat, stepping forward. 'Have you let that Prince's handsome face turn your head and shed what few wits you ever had? Don't you see what he is doing with this "modern" plan of his?'

'Actually, it wasn't his plan. It was my idea.' Elora had no idea why she'd even revealed that. Usually, it was best to just listen to what her mother had to say, but the words had stung.

'I don't believe that for a minute, but if it is true then you are an even bigger fool than I thought you were. You have played straight into his hands. Do you really believe he will marry you now?'

Elora stared at her mother. 'I don't understand.'

'Then let me explain.'

CHAPTER SIX

THE FOLLOWING DAY, Rohan looked at the text he'd received three hours after leaving Elora the previous evening, not from Elora herself but from a 'royal events coordinator', asking him to meet the royal family for a 'meet and greet', followed by official photographs, prior to leaving with Elora for a visit to a mango farm. After a tour there, Elora would return to the palace and then he would take her for dinner.

At least he'd insisted on arranging the dinner himself and he'd spent the morning doing exactly that.

He checked his phone again, aware of a wish that it had been Elora who had messaged him. He'd had a feeling the previous night that he shouldn't leave her, but what could he have done—whisked her away from her parents? On what grounds? The meeting had gone well and it was fair enough that the Queen had wanted to spend time with her daughter.

Yet unease lingered, however irrational, and

remained with him as the official car drove up to the steps of a side entrance to the palace, leading to a pillared patio area where the royal family awaited him.

Official photographers were already in place, his arrival recorded with all due pomp and ceremony, and he forced himself to smile as he climbed out of the official car. He made his way up the sweeping stone steps and looked up to meet Elora's eyes and now his smile turned genuine, but even as his gaze rested on her he was aware of something…wrong.

Though he couldn't place it. She looked beautiful, her salwar kameez today a teal tunic patterned with the national bird of Caruli, a golden myna, over dark flared trousers. Her lips upturned in just the right way, the smile held the exact right mix of pleasure at seeing him, tempered by a hint of shyness. Just as a princess should look at someone who she might, just might, be attracted to, and who might, just might, be attracted back.

The illusion was perfect but it was wrong, however right it looked. Or he was completely overreacting and overthinking—that was also a possibility, but his instincts, honed by years of ambassadorial and diplomatic duties, were usually pretty spot-on. But the important thing was it looked right and he wouldn't be the one to mess it up.

He smiled again and turned to the Queen, who touched her hand to his shoulder in the traditional greeting that granted a level of familiarity. The cameras clicked one last time before staff members ushered the press away to give the family some privacy. Queen Joanna waited, then gestured to a young woman standing next to her.

'This is Her Royal Highness Princess Flavia, mother to Prince Viraj.'

Rohan studied Elora's sister, or half-sister to be precise, and could see a superficial resemblance, though the two women were completely different. Flavia's glossy black hair was pulled back in a bun, her eyes dark brown, though she shared her sister's long dark lashes. Like Elora, her expression was regal and remote but her eyes held a tinge of bitterness he recognised all too well. He'd seen the same expression in the mirror during his marriage breakup. Rumours had circulated about the state of the royal Carulian marriage, but the speculation had died or been killed off and on the surface all was well between the couple—he hoped that was the truth. He smiled now, greeted Flavia and then turned to the dark-haired boy next to her, solemn-faced and upright despite being only five years old.

Rohan grinned at him, recalled being five,

being the heir and being on show. 'I am very pleased to meet you. Are you coming with us today? I bet you'd love to climb a mango tree and pick some mangoes.'

The little boy's face lit up, just as Rohan realised that was the wrong thing to say—he could sense the disapproval radiating like a laser from the Queen. And so could Viraj, as after one swift look at his grandmother he shook his head.

'I am sorry, I cannot. I have lessons this afternoon.'

'Plus climbing trees is not what princes do,' the Queen said.

Rohan thought that Flavia was going to say something, saw Elora step closer to her half-sister, and instead Flavia pressed her lips together and put a gentle hand on her son's head.

'Perhaps another day we can do something different,' he suggested. 'Something we can all agree on.'

'I would like that,' the little boy said, but Rohan sensed from his tone he had no expectation of it actually happening.

'So would I,' he said firmly. 'Let's shake on it.'

Viraj smiled and stuck his hand out to shake Rohan's, before stepping back to stand by his mother. Rohan caught Elora's eye and she smiled at him.

A real smile this time and it caught him unawares, froze him to the spot.

'The carriage is here.' The Queen's words
broke the spell and he turned automatically,
aware that the photographers would be back and
taking pictures in earnest. In that second, before the photographers approached, he saw the
Queen take Elora's wrist in a quick grasp, lean
forward and whisper something, her expression
retaining a smiling serenity.

But, whatever she said, it caused Elora dis-
tress, the look of resignation, sadness and weary
acceptance fleeting but definite, and then it was
gone as she stepped forward towards him, towards the waiting phalanx of photographers.
There she was next to him, and awareness of her
proximity tightened his gut. He glanced at her
once, saw that she looked relaxed as she faced
the cameras, yet he sensed a tension in her body
as she waved and smiled.

The tinkling of bells indicated the arrival of
the horse and carriage and within seconds a lavishly ornate carriage appeared, the body black
and gilded with gold leaf, the massive wheels
also lined with gold, the two horses a glossy
ebony black, their manes plaited, their bridles
glinting gold in the sunshine. The turbaned
driver was perched high at the front.

As he pulled the horses to a smooth stop in

front of them, Elora stiffened, her whole body taut, but she continued forward and Rohan was sure no one else would have seen her very slight hesitation. But something was going on, he just didn't know what. Wasn't sure if it was her mother's words, the sheer symbolic enormity of taking the first step of their fake story, the first step towards a marriage of duty, or the mass of photographers.

As they approached the carriage he nodded the staff member away and held out his hand for Elora so he could help her in, saw surprise flash in her eyes, followed by a gleam of appreciation as the cameras clicked around them.

And yet he hadn't done it for the cameras but because he'd sensed that she was troubled. Once seated, she smiled a lovely smile at the driver.

'Hello, Jaswant. Thank you so much for being here.'

'You're welcome, Your Highness. The journey should be about twenty minutes.'

Twenty minutes spent looking out at the lined streets, smiling, waving... The whole thing, as always, made Rohan feel slightly ridiculous. Though he made sure to keep a lookout to assess the level of support, and noted a few in the crowd holding anti-monarchy placards.

In the promised twenty minutes they arrived at their destination and Elora turned to him.

'Ready?' he asked.

'Ready.'

This time he waited as someone came to the door to let Elora out, watched as she descended gracefully with a friendly smile, and then his door was open and he stepped down, braced himself for more photographs, tried to offer a smile that held enough charm to bely his reputation of being cold and unfeeling without looking as if he was trying too hard.

Before he could figure out if he had it right or not, Elora had made her way to his side and, in an easy gesture that looked completely natural, she took his arm and gave him the smallest of pinches. Hell, it took him by surprise but it worked, focused him, as she smiled and beckoned the press forward.

'Hey guys, just to let you know I'll be showing Prince Rohan around Caruli over the next few days and he'll be returning the favour in Sarala. I'll make sure you're kept informed of our official itinerary. So we're going in here for a private tour for a couple of hours then back to the palace. Whilst I have you all here, can I also say how glad I am to be showing the Prince one of our best, high-quality exports. When we leave here, I know Pria and Kamal, owners of this lush farm, will have made sure Prince Rohan is an expert on organic mango farming and a definite fan of their mangoes in particular.'

'I'm looking forward to it,' Rohan said. 'And also looking forward to showing Princess Elora Sarala.'

With that, they made their way towards the farm entrance and, once inside, Elora led the way to an open paved courtyard enclosed by a low roofed farmhouse, the brick walls topped with terracotta roof tiles.

'This looks almost Mediterranean,' he said.

'It's all eco-friendly,' Elora replied. 'The bricks are actually made from local soil, and Kamal got the tiles second-hand from a local builder when someone was replacing their Mediterranean roof. There's no cement so that water drainage can be maximised—Kamal and Pria have done loads of courses in how to run a farm on ecological principles, so they are experts on utilising rain harvesting strategies. All the spaces in the paving have been carefully thought out.'

'That's impressive,' Rohan said, looking around with interest.

A woman who Rohan estimated to be in her fifties emerged from the front door and headed towards Elora, a beaming smile of welcome on her face as she embraced her in a massive hug, one Elora returned with fervour, before turning to Rohan.

'This is Pria, my old nurse.'

'Less of the old, missy.' The woman turned to Rohan and gave him a long appraising look before turning back to Elora, her expression neutral and, not for the first time, he wished that people wouldn't judge him by his reputation. 'I spoke to your mother,' she said. 'The Queen instructed me that you should take Rohan round the farm on your own.' Pria hesitated, glanced at Elora's set expression and back to Rohan. 'But if you'd rather have some company then I am happy to come along.'

Elora smiled but shook her head. 'It's fine. I don't know anywhere near as much as you, but I can give Rohan some information.'

'Then you head straight back. The whole family want to see you and I'll have freshly made mango smoothie all ready.'

'That sounds amazing,' Rohan said. 'I'd love to hear more about the way you run the farm.'

Pria eyed him with evident scepticism in her brown eyes and Rohan nodded firmly, wanting to show this woman, whom he instinctively liked, that he wasn't the monster she believed him to be.

'Really.' Rohan glanced around. 'I am genuinely interested. I was wondering if you'd ever thought about inviting guests, paying guests, to see what you do. You've got the space to build accommodation and I think people would be genuinely interested. Just like I am,' he added for good measure.

That got the very smallest of smiles. 'I think that's a good idea; I just haven't managed to persuade my husband. Yet. I'd be happy for you to say your bit.' She turned back to Elora. 'You sure you don't want me to come?'

'I'm sure. I'll be fine.'

She'd be fine, fine, fine. Elora didn't feel fine. She was dreading this conversation—a conversation her mother had instructed her must happen, the order given. Last night, she had been convinced that her mother was right, that Elora had been a fool, a dupe, a pawn...but now, in Rohan's presence, it didn't seem as clear-cut. Which was ridiculous and proved her mother's point—maybe he was messing with her head.

For a while they walked in silence, a silence she appreciated as she let the familiar scents and sights soothe her mind, bring her a semblance at least of calm. The walk past the long earthy enclosure where Pria kept her hens and roosters, the brightly coloured birds each with their own individuality clawing the ground as they strutted about, clucking at intervals. Then past the cattle and alongside the small lake, a habitat for wild birds that skimmed the silver-blue water, under the overarching branches of the massive banyan tree.

Then they entered the lush beauty of the mango orchard and Elora inhaled the sweet scent of the nearly ripe fruit, interlaced with the turpentine nuance of the dark green leaves. Looked up at the spread of the trees dotted with the pink and yellow of the mangos. Rohan too gazed and she sensed his interest as well as his appreciation of the sight and smells.

'They should be harvesting,' she said. 'But they gave the pickers a few hours off to ensure our privacy.' She gestured upwards. 'They use the leaves as well—though I am not completely sure about the details of how they are picked. They have been used for medicinal reasons for centuries—apparently, if you burn them, the smoke gets rid of hiccups and is good for sore throats. And they are a source of Vitamin C, and they are great for cooking. Pria makes a wonderful chutney.'

She paused to take a breath. She knew she was rambling because she was nervous, and dreading the prospect of the conversation ahead. She wanted to talk about the beauty of their surroundings, to forget the doubts and bitterness of her conversation with her mother.

'Pria uses the mature leaves to make a *torana*, or gateway, at the entrance to the farmhouse.

They are supposed to bring good fortune because of their cleansing energy.'

'You're close to Pria, aren't you?' Rohan asked.

'Yes, I am. Pria has been…good to me.' She had been the only one who hadn't changed towards Elora after Sanjay's death, the only one who'd still loved and cared for her and tried to understand Elora's searing loss and grief. But not even Pria knew the full truth about that day—if she did, perhaps she would not have been so sympathetic. 'She liked you,' she added.

'Really?' Scepticism came across loud and clear.

'Really. She wouldn't have let us do this unchaperoned otherwise.'

'Despite what your mother ordered?'

'Despite that,' Elora said. 'Pria is one of the few people who doesn't always listen to my mother. Unlike me and Flavia.' She turned to him. 'You were very good with Viraj. He liked you too.'

'I liked him. What do you think he'd like to do with us?'

Surprise warmed her and then the penny dropped.

'I guess whatever you think would be a good publicity stunt.'

Now he stopped and there was anger in his dark eyes. 'Excuse me?'

'Isn't that why you suggested it? Why you

were nice to him?' Doubt assailed her at her easy assumption as his frown intensified into a full-blown scowl.

'I wouldn't do that. Wouldn't use a five-year-old child who is already overexposed to the public by sheer dint of his birth. I meant that as a genuine offer—if Viraj wanted to spend some time kicking a football around or climbing a tree or any other "normal" five-year-old thing. That was it and I would strongly veto any publicity around the whole thing.'

There was absolutely no doubting the sincerity of his words and now she reached out and laid a hand on his arm. 'I'm sorry. I jumped to an obviously wrong conclusion.'

'Why?'

Because that was what her mother had told her, had grabbed her wrist and told her not to be fooled by a man proven to be a cold, ruthless monster.

But how to say that? So, instead, 'Because everything we do, every smile, every word is an illusion. That's why I spent two hours last night researching the best way to flirt and use body language that implies attraction.'

'I appreciate that, and I agree that everything *we* do in public is an illusion, but not the words I say to a five-year-old child. And not the words we speak to each other in private. Everything I have said to you in private has been honest.'

But how could she believe that when her mother's words were still ringing in her ears?

'Yesterday I thought we'd at least taken the first steps towards trust. So what has happened since then? Did your mother say something in your mother-daughter chat?'

Elora could see no real point in prevarication, knew this conversation had to happen.

'Yes.'

'What did she say?'

Now she came to a halt, stood under a branch weighted with the round, luscious fruits.

'She wants me to tell you we need to announce the engagement now.'

She expected him to ask her why, what her mother's reasons were. Instead, he reached out and gently tipped her chin up so their gazes met, the touch fleeting and gentle and sending her spinning.

'What do *you* want?' he asked.

Elora's eyes widened in shock. No one ever asked her what she wanted. 'I don't know. I don't know what to think.'

'OK. How about we try to figure it out?'

She nodded, felt a sense of shyness. 'There's a place we can sit. It's where the pickers stop for a rest.' Minutes later, they were seated on a bench that surrounded one of the circular wooden tables, placed in a clearing at the edge of the orchard.

Rohan turned to face her. 'So what's going on?'

'My mother thinks you're playing me.' A memory of Queen Joanna's contemptuous expression loomed.

He thought for a moment and then shook his head. 'I may be being obtuse, but I don't get it.'

Neither had she at first. 'She thinks you aren't announcing the engagement because you're hedging your bets. That there's a high risk you'll string me along then back out, leaving me looking a fool.'

'But why would I do that?'

What to say to that?

Her mother's voice was in her ear.

'Get real, Elora. The more he gets to know you, the less likely he is to marry you. He's used to women of a different ilk. What if his last girlfriend turns up? Marrying a non-royal is suitably modern, isn't it?'

The words had been venomous.

'The thing Sarala needs most is an heir. Rohan may well decide he's better off with a beautiful Hollywood celebrity. Like his first wife, like his girlfriends. Women you can't hope to live up to.'

Elora couldn't, wouldn't, repeat those words verbatim.

'Because you may get a better offer,' she said. 'Or find someone better suited to being Queen. Or your parents may find you a better option.'

'That won't happen. I spoke with my parents last night—they very much want this marriage and they completely bought into the "romance" idea. Not just my parents but my sister too. Marisa loved the modernisation idea, and using our romance to get out and about. So I'm sure she'll have some "date" ideas for us.'

Elora blinked, tried and failed to imagine the Carulian royal family having the type of conversation Rohan was describing.

'OK. I accept your family are on board right now. But things change.' She looked towards the tree opposite them, the tree she and Sanjay had used to climb. 'Or…you may decide not to get married. You don't want to get married—you told me that yourself. If things look like they are stabilising on Sarala if the backlash isn't as we feared, then you might decide you can afford to wait for a while.'

She looked at him now, braced for…she wasn't sure what. Anger? Agreement? But all she saw was a serious look of intent.

'Do you really think I would do that to you?'

She met his gaze full-on. 'You are the one that said it isn't personal. So would Sarala do that to Caruli?'

To her surprise, he gave a sudden smile. 'Touché. But, as far as I'm concerned, I have made a commitment to you. *And* Sarala has made a commitment to Caruli. I won't walk away from that. I won't break my word.'

'Even if a better bride comes along?'

'Even then. Once a deal is made, it is made… I would like to think my word means something.'

But did it? That was the question. There was the Queen's voice again.

'He has shown the worth of his word with his first marriage. He is not a man to be trusted; I am sure Princess Caro would vouch for that. You need to secure him fast.'

As if reading the doubt on her face, he shrugged. 'Clearly, it doesn't.' The words were said lightly but she sensed that the idea hurt. He thought for a moment, his expression unreadable. 'How about I share a secret? Not anything soul-baring, but something important. A goodwill gesture.'

Elora looked at him; she knew what her mother would say—that it was a meaningless gesture. But she didn't believe that—could sense that sharing a confidence on any level wouldn't come easy to him. But they had to start somewhere and he was willing to make that start. That had to mean something.

She nodded. 'OK. Tell me a secret.'

Rohan leant forward slightly, rested his forearms on the table, and she was suddenly oh, so aware of him, the bulk of his body that exuded strength, the sheer clean, muscular lines of him, the swell of sculpted biceps under his shirt, the solid shape of his thighs next to hers. The canopy of the trees, the smell of the mangoes and the warm heat of the Carulian sun.

'So…' he said, and stopped. 'Very few people know this.'

'For what it's worth, you have my word that whatever you are going to tell me I will keep confidential. Completely.'

'Yesterday you told me a bit about your dream—about what you'd do if you weren't a princess, your alternative life. Well, this is about mine.' Now her attention was completely caught and she looked at him, willed him to keep talking. He inhaled deeply and then, 'I've set up my own business,' he said and she could hear pride in his voice even as he gave a small self-deprecating laugh. 'It's not a global multi-million venture or anything, though I wish I could make it into one, but it's a solid, profitable enterprise.'

'Tell me.'

'I haven't done it as a prince, I've done it as Rohan Carmody and so far, through various legal loopholes and thanks to a couple of trustworthy business partners, I've hidden my name and identity as much as it is possible to do. I know

I can't keep it secret for ever, but it was important to me to see if I could do it, and I knew my parents wouldn't approve. Wouldn't believe that a prince could also be a businessman. Wouldn't see the point in starting a venture I won't be able to continue, a venture that has nothing to do with Sarala.' There was resignation in his voice and she felt a pang of sympathy, understood all too well. 'So, there you are. That's my secret.'

'You can't leave it there. Tell me more. What sort of business is it? What are your plans for it? How did you start it?'

'You really want to know?'

'Of course I do. I am full of admiration.' The idea that Rohan wanted something more than the role allotted to him by fate, had actually got it together to do something about it was admirable. More than that, it was relatable, made her feel closer to him. The real him.

'It's a tourism business. When I was sent abroad as an ambassador it was to promote Saralan produce, improve our trade links, win more lucrative export deals for our silks. Make our small island more global, more well known. I enjoyed it, enjoyed the negotiations, and doing something for Sarala that I'm actually good at.'

Elora couldn't help but wonder if that had been a reference to his disastrous marriage and the negative publicity or something deeper.

'But I also realised I loved the travelling aspect of the job, I loved exploring different places and cultures and I was lucky, I got to do it as a prince and experience the most fabulous resorts and hotels on offer. But because I'm not that well known I could also sometimes be an ordinary person, a tourist who mingled with everyone else.'

'So you became interested in tourism?'

'Yes. It all started because I got to thinking how much more Sarala has to offer. And I wondered why we don't offer more tourism opportunities, given how much money it can generate for the economy. It all got me thinking, but then I realised I didn't really know anything about the tourism industry at all. So I figured I needed to find out more.

'I did a lot of research and I went and spoke to people who know what they are talking about. That is a perk of being a prince—it opens doors. I spoke to hotel magnates and government ministers and I got more and more interested in the idea.

'And then I was travelling somewhere and we passed an old rundown hotel and there was something about it—it looked like an opportunity to put some of the things I'd learnt to the test. Could I create a place where people would want to stay?'

'And did you?'

'Yes. And I loved every minute of it. It was an old rundown building but it had such amazing potential and it was…exhilarating. Costing it, getting the necessary finance, planning, designing…and I got involved in the actual building work. Knocking walls down, gutting rooms.'

As he spoke, Elora could picture it, imagine him, dark hair dust-covered and tousled, hammering, pounding, getting his hands dirty in a way princes were never supposed to. And watching him relive the experience sent a funny little buzz through her, seeing his face relaxed, his deep voice full of enthusiasm and pride.

'Then there was the marketing, the planning—I loved watching the hotel transform and take off.'

'Can I see it? Do you have pictures? A website?'

'Sure.' They shifted closer as he pulled out his phone. 'So this is what it looked like before.' And as he scrolled through the pictures, talked her through the transformation, she sensed his utter dedication to the project, to the business.

'I love it. Each room is so unique and yet they are all equally beautiful and they all have a little twist. The chandeliers in room seven are breathtaking and I love the rooftop room, with a porthole to the stars.' She reached out to enlarge the picture and her fingers brushed his and she couldn't withhold the small gasp, triggered by the sudden rush through her body. Now she realised how close they had somehow got, so that all it would take was an infinitesimal shift to be pressed right up against him.

She should move away, but she didn't want to, his tantalising nearness too tempting, so instead she cleared her throat and managed to ask the next question. 'What about food? Can I see the menu? When I have time, I try to cook food from abroad but I never know if I manage to make it authentic and of course I end up adapting the recipes to use more local ingredients.' She was rambling but she couldn't help it, could sense the tension in his body too, saw the care he used as he pressed the requisite buttons on his screen, angled the phone so she could see it.

'We do theme weekends,' he said. 'Not every weekend, but say for Halloween or Christmas or Independence Day…'

She read the menu out loud. 'The Valentine's menu features aphrodisiac ingredients, beautifully prepared with sizzle and spice and includes oyster risotto, chilli foie gras and a decadent dessert to share, complete with dark chocolate, passion fruit and a hint of ginger to hot things up.' There was a silence and then, she couldn't help it, she started to laugh and, seconds later, he followed suit.

'What were the chances of me randomly selecting that menu?' he asked, shaking his head. 'I'm sorry.'

'Don't be. I can't remember the last time I laughed like that.'

'Me neither.'

And there it was again. As their gazes met she was oh, so aware of him, his closeness, the planes of his face, the dark intensity of his eyes, which were fixed on her now, scrutinising her with such intent she gave a small shiver and somehow, with a sense of utter inevitability, they both moved at the same time.

Then, before she could even think about what she was doing, their lips met and for a glorious moment she was lost in a tumult of unfamiliar, unexpected pleasure. Dizzying sensations flooded her as her lips parted and he deepened the kiss, evoking a yearning need she'd never felt before.

That realisation trickled through the vortex of feelings, enough to trigger an escalation of panic. What was she doing? She had no idea. Couldn't fathom the depth of these exquisite needs that twisted her stomach, made her want to throw caution to the wind. *Oh, God.* Had she made a complete fool of herself? Rohan was an experienced man—for him, a kiss would mean noth-ing, was simply a way of passing the time. Now, he would know for sure what he could only have suspected—the extent of her inexperience—and mortification burned.

From somewhere there also burned a deter-mination to ensure damage limitation, to some-how keep the tattered remains of her dignity. Finding her inner strength, she pushed down the surge of desire with relentless force, focused on the tree she and Sanjay had once climbed, on the vista that reminded her of childhood lost, and she found if not true calm, then the ability to project it.

She shook her head. 'Turns out you don't need to actually taste the Valentine's menu to break the rules. I did promise not to plaster myself all over you on the first date—looks like we didn't make it that far. But probably best if we don't do that again when so little has been decided.'

What would her mother say? She could hear the light contemptuous laugh in her head, the sarcastic applause.

He played that well, distracted you with a tiny bit of charm and you're putty in his hands. For God's sake don't let the man seduce you before he dumps you.

She rose to her feet. 'Thank you for trusting me, your secret is safe with me, and now we'd better get back to Pria. The mango smoothies will be ready.' She managed what she hoped was a light laugh. 'And on the way back I'd better tell you something about mango farming.'

CHAPTER SEVEN

ROHAN KNEW HE should say something, do something, but as he rose to his feet all ability to speak seemed to have deserted him as he tried to figure out what the hell had just happened. He hadn't planned to kiss Elora; it had been the very last intention on his mind. The whole idea had been not to spook her by seeing if their attraction was real.

Well…that was out of the window, but it wasn't Elora who was acting spooked. It was him, because the unplanned kiss had blown his mind and his senses out of the water. And now…now he wasn't sure what was going on. One minute he'd been gloriously kissing her, the next she'd withdrawn and had swept the entire kiss under the proverbial carpet. Was hotfooting it back through the trees at a rate of knots, talking about mango farming as if she were a bona fide tour guide.

'Elora. Stop.'

She broke off.

'I am genuinely interested in this, but…'

'There are no buts. We are about to spend time with Pria and her husband and they will expect me to have told you something about the farm they are so justly proud of.'

'I get that and I've done the research. I spent a couple of hours last night getting some facts. So I can tell you that the farm aims to be self-sufficient as well as produce tonnes of produce per year for sale. They also produce bananas, lychees and many other fruits, they grow vegetables and spices and are renowned for their organic and eco methods. I want to discuss all this with Pria and I would really like to talk to them about how they could expand, have paying guests who learn from them and have an amazing experience. But, right now, that isn't what I want to talk about.'

'That's why we're here,' she said flatly.

'Perhaps we should have thought of that ten minutes ago. When we definitely were not talking about mangoes or anything else. I think we should talk about the kiss.'

For a surreal moment he thought she would ask, *What kiss?* Then, instead, 'I don't think it is worth discussing.'

'Because it was so displeasing to you?' he asked, stung.

'Because it shouldn't have happened. For all

I know, you kissed me to mess with my head, distract me, confuse me…' She broke off.

Anger flashed through him that she could believe that, after what they'd shared, after the laughter, after he'd told her about his business, and then the anger morphed into a pang of hurt and an alarm bell rang at the back of his head. What was going on here? Anger, hurt, laughter…kisses. This was spiralling into emotions he had no wish to feel. This marriage was not supposed to be emotional—he would not step onto that rollercoaster again. But neither would he let this go. He could see the confusion, the wariness in her grey eyes. And he understood—her mother had planted seeds of doubt in her mind and he couldn't blame Elora for believing them. He knew his reputation was hardly stellar.

'That kiss was unplanned. I shared a confidence with you in good faith in the hope it would demonstrate that I am on the level. I have no wish to mess with either of our heads. All I want is to get on with this charade and complete our deal for the sake of our countries. You can choose to believe that or not. I truly hope you do, but I do understand that you may have reservations. It's your call.'

Elora closed her eyes and took a deep breath. 'I'm sorry,' she said simply. 'You did trust me and I truly appreciate that and what you told me.

As for the kiss, it's unfair of me to dump all the blame on you… I was there too. And you're right. I need to decide—so I say let's stick to the plan. I don't think announcing the engagement now is the right idea. But perhaps as well as evaluating in two weeks time we can tell my parents we plan to announce the engagement in a month.' She gave a small smile, but he sensed it was a genuine attempt to call a truce. 'Does that sound fair?'

A temporary trust earned and a compromise that would hopefully satisfy her mother. That made sense.

'Agreed. And Elora?'

'Yes?'

'I promise that kiss was not planned. I didn't mean to mess with your head or make things more complicated. I'm sorry.' For a moment he relived that kiss, the sheer unbridled, glorious joy of it, 'But it is hard to regret something so…enjoyable.' The word didn't do it justice, but somehow he needed to keep it in perspective. It was a kiss.

She bit her lip, looked down and then back up again, slowly unclenched her hands and nodded. 'Then I guess the best thing we can do is put it behind us.'

'That sounds like an idea.' Though he wasn't sure how easy that was going to be. It felt to him as though Pandora's box had been opened, and once open it couldn't be closed again. There was no way he was forgetting that kiss in a hurry.

'Now we really had better go,' Elora said. 'Pria's mango smoothies are worth hurrying for. She puts a secret ingredient in that she won't tell me and...' She gave a sudden smile. 'If you can convince Kamal that paying guests are a good idea Pria will love you for ever. Then after that we need to prepare for our dinner date. Where are we going?'

He smiled at her,, suddenly aware of a sense of anticipation, one he tried to damp down. It was just dinner. Just like the kiss had been just a kiss. In which case, why was his body still taut, his gut still clenched with desire, his mind still blown? 'It's a surprise,' he said.

Elora was none the wiser a few hours later, as she surveyed her wardrobe and tried to figure out what on earth a sheltered princess should wear on a surprise first date.

She closed her eyes and tried to pretend this was real—that Rohan had asked her on a genuine date. If the illusion was real. If that kiss had been to him what it had been to her. To Rohan, it had meant nothing apart from an unplanned 'enjoyable' moment. He'd been unaffected, able to impress Pria and Kamal, and discuss the prospect of expanding the farm's business with an enthusiasm she now understood. Tourism was something that Rohan genuinely felt a passion for.

Whereas the kiss had meant nothing—to him, such kisses were commonplace. After all, he would have experienced hundreds, if not thousands, of kisses that had been way more 'enjoyable' with women he'd *wanted* to be with, not a woman he was stuck with through duty.

But to Elora the kiss had been…magical, a few minutes of sheer new sensations that had unlocked a part of her she'd never known existed. Which was mortifying. In the extreme. And yet here she was thinking about it again and now a sudden sense of defiance touched her.

It was true that she'd never be a woman he'd choose to marry, but dammit, she could maybe at least make him believe kissing her would be better than 'enjoyable'. She closed her wardrobe door with a decisive thud and frowned, thought for a moment and then pulled her phone from her pocket and texted a message. A few minutes later she was heading along the corridor towards the three-bedroom annexe where Flavia resided.

She wondered, hoped, she'd made the right decision. She and Flavia weren't close, but they had never really had the chance. Flavia had lived with her mother after the King had divorced his first wife, and Elora had seen her older half-sister only rarely. Then Flavia had been recalled to the palace when Elora was seventeen and soon after that she had been married, and a year after that Viraj was born.

In that time Elora had wanted to get to know Flavia better, but somehow nothing had ever come of it. Her mother had told Elora that Flavia blamed Queen Joanna for the divorce and that resentment extended to Elora.

But instinct told Elora her mother was wrong, and now she was putting that to the test, asking her sister for help. As she approached her sister's quarters, Flavia pulled the door open.

'Hi.'

'Hi.'

They both spoke together and Elora gave a slightly nervous laugh in the ensuing silence as each studied the other.

'I'm glad you messaged,' Flavia said.

'Really?'

'Really. Tell me what you need.'

'I need an outfit that will make me look as though I have dressed up for a date.'

'And you don't have anything like that?'

'No.'

'Because the Queen doesn't think you need it and the outfit you have in mind isn't one she would approve of?'

'Exactly. I want to look…attractive.'

'For Rohan?' There was no judgement in her sister's voice.

'I want him to notice me. Properly. Is that silly?'

'No, it isn't.' Flavia reached out, laid a hand on Elora's arm. 'I'm not sure what is going on between you and Rohan, but it seemed to me earlier that you have already got his attention.'

Elora sighed. 'Not really. He accepts he has to marry me and I think he is making the best of it, but just once I'd like him to see me as a person, not a Princess of Caruli.'

'I get that,' Flavia said, and there was both understanding and sadness in her voice, and for a moment Elora wondered if she was thinking about her own marriage. But, before she could ask, Flavia gave her head a small shake and then she smiled. 'I completely get it and I have just the right outfit in mind.'

Rohan was ushered into the Treasure Room and announced with due pomp and ceremony. He waited for the equerry to leave and stepped forward to greet Queen Joanna and Flavia.

'I am sure Elora will be here soon,' Flavia said in a soothing tone, and Rohan could swear she gave him the smallest of secret smiles as she scrutinised him.

'I expect my daughter to show punctuality,' the Queen said.

'Perhaps I am a little early,' Rohan replied, just as the door pushed open and he saw Pamir in the doorway, an especially wooden expression on his face.

'Her Royal Highness the Princess Elora,' he said and stood to one side.

Rohan heard a sudden almost choking sound and realised it came from his throat. Dressed in a shimmering golden lehenga set, with a long swirling skirt and a cropped blouse that left her midriff bare, she looked... Elora looked... He couldn't come up with any adjectives, any words at all. For the first time he understood the cartoon characters whose eyes popped out on springs.

He continued to stare, saw her loose hair cascading in waves to touch her bare shoulders, bangles encircling her slim arms and a gauzy dupatta scarf complementing the whole, along with strappy jewelled sandals.

He blinked as Flavia cleared her throat meaningfully and he looked away and saw Queen Joanna's face. Well, Elora had surprised him, but, unfortunately, she had clearly also surprised her mother, whose face had screwed up into a look of utter displeasure. But, before she could speak, Flavia broke into speech.

'Elora, we were just wondering where you

were. I think Rohan is worried you'll be late. He has a reservation, but he won't tell us where.'

She moved towards Rohan as she spoke and gave him a small unseen nudge.

Somehow gathering himself, he nodded. 'Flavia is right. We'd better get moving. The car is waiting outside. The driver is my own personal security officer so Elora is in safe hands.' He spoke evenly but made sure there were no pauses as he ushered her towards the door. Elora swivelled and as he looked back he saw Flavia give them both the thumbs-up sign and then a shooing motion.

'I suggest we walk fast,' he said sotto voce and they half walked, half ran down the marble corridor, through the door and towards the waiting car. It was only once they were inside that she turned to look at him and he couldn't help it, he began to laugh and soon she joined in.

'I didn't think we'd make it out of there,' he said. 'So what's going on? I thought your mother was going to throw me out and forbid the date.'

'I borrowed the clothes from Flavia. My mother expected me to wear one of my more "usual" outfits. Not this.'

There was a silence and Rohan said softly, 'I like this.'

Suddenly, just like that, the car seemed to

shrink, the air seemed to thicken and his heart started to beat faster.

'Good. I thought it was more appropriate for the vibe we are trying to project,' she said hurriedly as if she too felt the tension in the car rise and simmer and she continued, her voice slightly breathless, 'I thought about it and if we want the press to take an interest and pick up the romance idea there is no point in me dressing the same way I always do. We want to demonstrate that we are no longer doing this for diplomatic reasons. This is a date, not a business dinner. It's personal. Dressing like this seems to mark a clear line between what I wore to the mango farm.'

'Well, whatever your reasons, you look stunning,' he said as the car glided to a stop. He pushed the intercom button. 'Thank you, Danzi. Fabulous driving, as always. I'll message you when we're ready to be picked up. If there are any press, we're going with option U.'

'What's option U?' Elora asked.

He answered in a murmur, after he'd walked round to open her door for her. 'The one where we are unusually polite. The alternative is option ST. Screw them.'

Elora smiled up at him just as the cameras flashed as she climbed out of the car.

But though he'd meant the words to hold humour, as he saw the press surge in, memories of past encounters threatened and, as if she sensed it, she kept her hand on his arm as they turned to the cameras and the bombardment of questions.

'So what's happening? Is this a business dinner? Or a date?'

'No comment,' Rohan said, and she gently pressed down on his forearm, forced him to stop as she spoke to the journalists.

'Ask us tomorrow. We may have figured it out by then,' she said lightly, and smiled at the reporter. 'And watch this space,' she added as she pressed his arm again and they started to move towards the restaurant door.

CHAPTER EIGHT

ROHAN INHALED DEEPLY. 'You handled that well.'

'Not really. The press have always been kind to me, so it wasn't hard.'

She glanced towards the hustle and bustle of the busy restaurant, where heads were already turning. 'This bit will be more difficult for me,' she added, 'Whereas you are most used to it. Being the centre of attention with a date, in a multi star restaurant.'

'Actually,' he said, 'I have it planned a little differently.'

Elora was right. Back in New York or London, or wherever he'd been staying, he had got used to wining and dining women in a public setting, had been adept at using that publicity to promote Sarala as best he could. But here, today, he had no wish to be on show.

He turned to smile at the proprietor, a man in his thirties, with trademark slicked back dark hair and a beaming smile. 'Rohan.'

'Michel.' Not that he had originally been called

that, but it was the name the public knew him by and, whilst he wasn't a global name, he was definitely famed throughout this part of Asia.

'Everything is ready for you and the Princess.'

Elora beamed. 'I can't believe I'm meeting you. I am star-struck—I have always wanted to come here and I loved your latest book. Your take on a chicken *cafreal* was absolutely incredible.'

Michel beamed. 'I am overseeing your food myself,' he said. 'But now follow me.'

He led them away from the dining room and Elora turned an enquiring glance to Rohan, who smiled what he hoped was an enigmatic smile. To his own surprise, anticipation swelled inside him as they climbed the spiral staircase and he realised he was looking forward to seeing Elora's reaction. He tried to tell himself this was all an illusion, but knew he wanted, hoped, to bring a real smile to her face, the one that sparked her eyes and also narrowed them ever so slightly, wanted her to see that he too had put some thought into their date this evening.

Once again, a warning bell clanged in the back of his head, but this time he shut it down. There was nothing wrong with wanting to be nice.

They reached the top of the stairs and stepped out onto the terrace, bathed in the golden rays of the evening sun. Leading to their table, by the side of the surrounding stone wall, there was an arched trellis, woven with a selection of foliage and bright flowers he'd chosen from the local flower market. Teals and pinks mixed against dark green to show the colours of the Carulian flag, alongside whites and reds to represent the colours of Sarala. The table itself was placed to optimise the view of the waterfront, the dark blue of the sea glinting with silver against the deep golden yellow of the sand. It was simply but beautifully set, the glass top strewn with flower petals.

Elora looked around, wide-eyed, and then gave a small gasp. 'It's beautiful.'

'I can't take credit for this,' Michel said with a note of regret. 'This was all Rohan. I told him I would offer him a job.'

'It's magical,' she said. And the smile she turned to him was all Rohan could have hoped for.

'There is a cocktail all ready for you with some snacks. The first course will arrive shortly.'

With that, Michel left and they walked over to the table.

'Mango margarita,' Rohan said as he handed her a glass. 'Made with a mango given to me by Pria.'

'Really?'

'Really. I told you, I am a man of my word.'

'That makes this extra special.' She sipped the drink and gave an appreciative sigh. 'Perfect.' She gestured around. 'All of this is perfect.' She reached for her phone. 'It will look amazing on social media, a perfect setting for the charade.'

'Wait.' He reached out to move her hand out of the way and they both stopped at the touch, looked at each other across the small circular table, tension shimmering in the warm evening breeze as the sun began its descent, casting a deep glow across the sky.

Now he couldn't help but remember their kiss. How could he not, when she was so close, when he could smell her perfume, when he could see the satin sheen of her bare shoulders, the delicate planes and shadows of her collarbone, and his fingers tingled with a desire to run over the delicate contour, to drop kisses on the bare skin to provoke again that wonderful, glorious, joyous response?

He forced himself to stay still, not to spook her, but there was an answering flare in her grey eyes and a slight quiver in her body as she too fought to remain still.

'Yes?' she said, her voice a little breathless.

He held her gaze, held the moment. 'You're right, this will look good on social media, but I didn't just do it for that. I did it for you. I picked the flowers in the market with you in mind.'

Had even tried to match the scents to the elusive, tantalising perfume she wore. 'That's the truth as well.'

'Then thank you. You got it dead right. It's all I could have wanted from a first date.' She gave a small laugh. 'Even a pretend one.'

Before he could reply, he saw the door to the terrace swing open and a waiter appeared, balancing a tray.

Rohan welcomed the interruption, not sure what he would have said next, because right now this didn't feel fake. He wasn't sure how it felt.

Elora smiled up at the waiter, clearly also relieved by the distraction, the chance to change the mood, and soon she was engrossed in a discussion on the starters, a selection of snacks chosen to go with the cocktail.

The waiter left with a promise to return with the main course and the 'perfect wine' to go with it.

'These look perfect,' Elora said.

So do you. He bit back the words, aware of how cheesy they would sound.

'Tell me about them.'

'Weren't you listening?'

'No,' he admitted. He'd been too busy watching her, seeing the expressions flitting across her face, the focus as she'd discussed ingredients and textures.

She gave him a slightly puzzled look and then pointed at the plate. 'So we have kachori puff pastry filled with a spiced onion filling and then fried. The main spices are the fennel seeds and the nigella seeds, so they will have a slightly bitter flavour offset by some chilli powder and then the sweet chilli chutneys to dip them in. We also have long green chilli peppers stuffed with potato and deep fried. And finally, another deep-fried offering, lentil vadas, with spinach, chillies and ginger.' And now Elora did reach for her phone. 'But before we start we need a picture with the cocktails and the remains of the sunset. Then we *need* to eat. I can't believe you managed to get a table here.'

'I didn't. I was a bit flummoxed until Michel mentioned they are thinking about renovating the terrace so they can expand. I asked to see it and came up with the idea.'

Elora picked up a stuffed chilli and took a bite. 'Well, when you taste this you'll be glad you did!'

He realised he was already glad, perhaps too glad. But he couldn't help but enjoy her appreciation of the food, the venue and the occasion. Watching her sample each savoury snack, he savoured her enjoyment more than the actual food itself. He had to get a grip; it was time to get this dinner at least a little on track.

'I thought we could use this opportunity to discuss the future,' he said. In part to reassure Elora that he was serious about their marriage, despite her mother's concerns. 'Use the time to look forward, make plans, set rules.'

'Rules?' Now the smile dropped from her face, her expression wary, and for a moment he regretted his words, steeled himself to continue.

'Yes.'

'I wasn't aware a marriage had rules as such. We've already agreed there will be no scandals or indiscretions, that we will be faithful. What other rules could there be?'

'Perhaps "rules" is the wrong word. Expectations would be better.' He would not make the same mistakes twice. With Caro, he'd made so many incorrect assumptions and she'd accused him of smothering her, crowding her, not giving her space. He'd got so much wrong; he wouldn't again.

'Our marriage is an agreement, a contract, and I want us to figure out the terms, what we both want from it, apart from a means to bring our countries together, apart from an heir.'

There was the slightest of pauses as she looked down to her empty plate, took the last sip of her cocktail.

'OK. That makes sense.' She looked up. 'I'll

pop to the bathroom and I'll have a think whilst the main course arrives.'

Elora looked at her reflection in the small private bathroom Michel had put aside for her use. Saw the sparkle in her eyes, looked down at what she was wearing, and knew she was in danger of letting an illusion mess with her head. For a while there, as they had sipped cocktails in the rays of the setting sun, it had felt all too real.

But it wasn't. This wasn't a romance. It was an arrangement and she knew she should be grateful that Rohan wanted to set some rules—rules he was consulting her on. It made sense. With rules in place, their marriage had a chance of being way more successful than so many marriages based on love. Expectations could be managed—she closed her eyes—or could they? Rohan was expecting an heir—what if that was an expectation she could not fulfil? She couldn't afford to think like that. Her worries were just that—worries, that might prove to be utterly unfounded. She couldn't jeopardise this agreement, which was so important for her country, because of a worry.

So now she would pull herself together. Go and set some rules.

By the time she returned to the table the main course was already in place.

Rohan smiled. 'The waiter said to tell you that Michel would be happy to discuss ingredients and methods with you later, and he is even willing to give you his personal email and number.'

'He may live to regret that.' Her smile was friendly but cooler than before; she knew she had herself in hand now. 'So—the rulebook,' she said. 'Where do you want to start?'

'How about you tell me how you see your life once we are married?'

The question made reality loom; in a few months she would be married to the man opposite her, would have vowed to spend the rest of her life with him. She closed her eyes briefly and focused on this moment, concentrated on the taste of the food, the texture of the *appam*, the pancake served with the vegetable *ishtu*. She ran through the ingredients. Rice flour for the *appam*, coconut milk used in both *appam* and *ishtu*, the sauce spiced with cloves, cinnamon, coriander. The crunch of the cauliflower, cut into perfect bite-sized chunks, the potato, soft but not too soft.

Enough, Elora. Answer the question.

'I assume we will live on Sarala.'

He nodded. 'Yes. Though I am hoping to continue some of my ambassadorial duties, as well as keep an eye on my hotel. So I may spend some of my time abroad.' She waited, aware of a hope that he would suggest she travel with him. Instead, 'So you needn't be worried that you won't have your own space. You will. There are a number of royal residences we can live in—the one I have in mind has plenty of space so we can have separate quarters.'

Elora didn't understand why his words weren't making her happier. When the plan for this marriage had first been mooted she'd have been filled with relief at the idea of keeping everything as separate as possible.

She gave her head a small shake and looked up at him. 'That sounds ideal,' she said firmly. Rohan was giving her a chance to live her own life, something she had always wanted to do, and she would take the opportunity with both hands instead of letting a sunset mess with her head. 'I would also like some autonomy in other areas, though I will, of course, carry out all my royal duties. Do you have any idea what they will entail?'

'Similar, I imagine, to what your mother and sister carry out on Caruli. There will be royal visits, events, you will be on the board of various charities and take on other duties as they arise.'

Such as being a parent—mother to the heir of Sarala. The idea was not one she wanted to contemplate, and the guilty knowledge that it might not be that easy sent a burgeoning anxiety straight through her.

'That all sounds as I expected, but I would like to do more than that.'

'In what way? Do you want to get a job, pursue a career?'

'Not as such. I don't feel working for a salary when the royal family already holds so much wealth is necessarily fair, given I do not already have a career of my own. I meant I would like a more hands-on role than my mother has. Rather than being on the board of a charity I'd like to play a more active part.'

'I have the feeling you have something in mind.'

Elora hesitated. 'Yes, I do.' He said nothing, simply held her gaze, and she knew the choice now was hers. To trust him or not. He could do no more to advocate that trust than he had already done. She closed her eyes, put her mother's voice out of her mind and made that choice. This man was offering her a fair shot at a partnership. This was not, could never be, the marriage of fairy tales, but it could perhaps still be a happy union. 'But I'll need to explain, and to do that I will need to share a secret with you.'

'For what it's worth, you have my word that whatever you are going to tell me I will keep confidential. Completely.'

He'd echoed her own words of earlier back to her and she got the message. He'd trusted her, she needed to return the favour. And she would. 'Thank you. Because it's not just about me.' If he did betray her, she wasn't the only one who would be in trouble.

'Right, here goes.' She pushed her empty plate to one side, took a sip of wine and started.

'A few months ago, I was at an official function, a fashion show featuring a designer from Caruli, a protégé of my mother. During the show there was a protest; a woman ran into the event, brandishing a placard. The message was simple—she was saying that the cost of a single outfit would feed her family for a month.

'She was hustled out but…it made me think. My mother told me that it was sheer nonsense, that families like that needed to learn to budget better, manage better, and that Caruli is one of the most prosperous islands in the region. I knew that the latter fact was true, but that's all very well for the eighty-five percent of the population who are OK—what about the rest? I was also ashamed to realise I don't really know how much it costs to feed a family.'

'It's not your fault. How could you or I know? We aren't taught things like that.'

'Then we need to find out for ourselves. How can a royal family rule if they don't understand how real life works for most people?' She paused, suddenly aware of how passionate she sounded, knew that her parents would have deemed this conversation unseemly and closed it down, taken her words as an insult, an unacceptable criticism.

'You're right.' She looked at him almost suspiciously, the words so unfamiliar she thought there must be an edge to them. But he continued, leaning forward, and she could see real interest, that he was listening. 'So I take it you did some research.'

'Yes, I did. And that protester was right—her maths made sense. But I also learnt more about the fifteen percent of people who don't have enough money. I learnt about food banks and the struggle to get help and I have tried, really tried, to get to grips with it. Though I know how daft that sounds, sitting here at one of Caruli's best restaurant's sipping cocktails.'

'It doesn't sound daft. But I hope you don't feel guilty about it—you were born royal—that wasn't your choice and the lifestyle we have comes with the territory.'

'But it doesn't, or it shouldn't, come with the territory to ignore those who are struggling. So I decided I wanted to do something. However small.'

'What did you do?'

'I tried to think of something I could do in my capacity as princess, but my mother vetoed any involvement at all. She said I mustn't do anything political, especially when there was already unrest on Baluka. Mustn't "rouse the rabble".' Elora had disagreed so profoundly with her mother's words that for once she had nearly argued back, nearly shown some moral backbone. But in the end she'd simply bowed her head, whilst resolving to find a way. 'So I found a soup kitchen and I volunteered there as a private citizen called Preeti Bannerjee. They have no idea who I really am.'

Rohan stared at her. 'But how on earth have you pulled that off?'

'I have help from a member of staff who is also a friend.' She knew he would guess it was Pamir but she didn't name him. 'His wife lends me her clothes. We are a similar build. I even have a wig, a very realistic one, I may add. So I am a brunette rather than a blonde, I dress in jeans and a top, an outfit Princess Elora would never be seen in, and it works. Pamir covers for me and so far, it has worked. I help out, I cook—sometimes when I can I take the leftovers from the kitchens. I give as much of my money as I can without arousing suspicion and I love it.'

'Good for you. You are doing a good thing.' He leant back and lifted his glass. 'To Preeti Bannerjee. I hope to meet her one day.'

'It doesn't feel like I'm doing enough, though. I want to do more—and there is so much to do.

So I was thinking, hoping, that if…when we get married I could be more involved. Not as Preeti Bannerjee but as myself. Perhaps arrange charity fundraisers, try to raise awareness, if I can't continue with the more hands-on work. Unless, of course, your parents veto it.'

'They won't,' Rohan said. 'My sister Marisa has always been a champion of the less well-off inhabitants of Sarala.' He paused. 'Though with Marisa it's hard to tell if it's because she cares about their plight or she thinks the poor are more likely to be anti-royalty. Sarala is less prosperous than Caruli—Marisa has been telling my parents for a while that they need to think about the percentage of people who may feel they would be better off in a republic.'

Elora's attention was caught. 'So your parents listen to you and Marisa?'

'They probably listen to Marisa more than me, but yes, they listen. They don't always agree, but they will let us have our say.'

Elora tried to imagine that—parents who at least listened, paid attention, believed you had something to contribute.

'In this case,' Rohan said, 'I think they would welcome your involvement. You can discuss it with them over the next few days.'

'Yes.' Though in truth she couldn't imagine doing anything of the sort. She was nervous enough at the prospect of leaving for Sarala the next day, staying with King Hanuman and Queen Kaamini.

Rohan looked at her. 'Don't worry. My parents will welcome you. They are pleased the marriage is going ahead.'

Pleased that their son who had no wish to marry was willing to do his duty. Duty—that was all this was about. This charade. The reminder was perhaps opportune as the waiter brought out the dessert, a beautiful concoction of ice cream topped with strawberry meringues and tiny dark chocolate truffles, presented in a rose gold bowl for sharing, complete with two heart-shaped dessert spoons.

It was nothing but a prop, to sustain an illusion that masked a political necessity. And she mustn't forget that. Elora reached for her phone again, kept her voice cool and businesslike.

'So the plan is to leave for Sarala tomorrow afternoon, after we have a "romantic" picnic breakfast, and then spend some time with Viraj as planned. I thought we could do some baking; I think he'd like that. Also, that way, we're in the palace kitchens and no one can change it into a publicity stunt. That's the agenda.'

An agenda, the perfect word for a planned romance, an illusion that would melt away once the marriage was sealed. Melt away like the ice cream in front of them, and the glint from the heart-shaped spoons seemed to mock her as she took the picture.

CHAPTER NINE

ROHAN WOKE UP, stared up at the ceiling and re-alised he was smiling, realised too that he was looking forward to seeing Elora. With a frown, he swung his legs out of bed and headed to the bathroom. Yes, dinner had been enjoyable, but this was ridiculous. All of this was part of a plan, an agenda.

Half an hour later, he walked down the ma-jestic treelined avenue, the chinar trees covered in a dense foliage of verdant green, followed Elora's instructions and soon saw her kneeling under one of the trees, spreading a blanket on the ground. A picnic spot, chosen in the hope that one or more of the gardening staff would spot them and release a picture to social media.

As she saw him approach, she opened the wicker basket next to her, pulled out a container and opened it.

'That smells incredible,' he said.

'I've made *dosas* with a potato filling and to follow I've made a fruit salad. Hopefully, the kitchen staff will also have taken note and plenty of speculation will be swirling.'

'Good. I think so far, so good?'

'I hope so,' she said as she handed him a cup of coffee. 'But perhaps we should do a social media check.'

He nodded, pulled his phone out and started to scroll as he bit into the *dosa*. 'This is delicious.'

When she didn't respond, he turned and saw that she was intent on reading something.

'Elora?'

The sharpness of his tone penetrated her concentration. 'There's an article on Celebchat.' A massively popular site that covered hot celebrity gossip.

Quickly, he found it and started to read.

How does Princess Elora measure up? Let's check the Dateometer!

Rohan scanned the article under the headline, wondering how the reporter had unearthed the series of photographs, all of him on a series of first dates. A grainy old photo of him aged eighteen with a girl he barely even remembered, and then his first date with Caro. His twenty-three-year-old self was staring across a table, a ridiculous look on his face of adoration, obsession, utter absorption, and he flinched as he looked at it.

Caro had been two years older than him in age, and at least five years older in experience, already a well-known actress, a near household name, a friend of his sister. Marisa had asked Caro to 'look after him' and so she'd contacted him, then asked him out for dinner, and then everything had spiralled. She'd reeled him in, revelled in her all too easy conquest of him, used her undeniable ability to entice and promise and pull back and it had left him a quivering mess ruled by his hormones.

He pulled himself back from this trip down memory lane and turned his attention to the next photos. There he was, opposite a woman he'd dated for about six months, just after the divorce, a Hollywood actress. The next photo showed his most recent relationship, a model he'd gone out with for three months.

His expression in those photos was clearly posed for effect, his smile assured and charming, and his dates had been equally playing to the camera.

And then there were two photos with Elora, clicked as they were entering the restaurant and again when they came out. They were both smiling, and he tipped his head to study the images more clearly.

'I think we did OK,' he said. 'We're smiling, we look as though we like each other and...' He broke off, clocked how still she was before she turned to look at him.

'The photos are fine.'

Her voice was tight and he saw she was still staring at the screen and he followed suit, readi the article below. A quick précis on who each woman was, and then the conclusion.

> *There are no photos of our Princess on previous dates—this is her first foray into the world of dating. How will she fare?*
>
> *Our gallant Princess can hold out some hope that she measures up not too badly in the looks department...but does she have what it takes to hold Rohan's eye now she's caught it?*
>
> *What does this sheltered, inexperienced princess have that Princess Caro didn't?*
>
> *Can she compare to Hollywood royalty or the Queen of the catwalk?*
>
> *Only time will tell, but let us know what you think.*
>
> *Answer the poll: Does Princess Elora have what it takes?*

Rohan looked up, saw the set expression on Elora's face and thought carefully about his next words.

'I think we could have come off worse than

this and in fact I am sure that we will as this "romance" progresses.' He was counting his lucky stars they hadn't delved into his previous marriage in any detail, hadn't regurgitated all the old stories and scandals.

'I know it could have been worse.' But her voice was colourless. 'Plus it is irrelevant. We will marry whatever the poll says.'

'A poll that will be carried out by people who know none of the "contestants",' he pointed out. 'Plus the very fact the poll exists proves that people already believe in our romance. That's a good thing, right?'

'Yes,' she agreed. 'So far, so good. So let's get on with our day. Would you like some fruit salad?'

'Sure.'

But as they ate, despite the fact that Elora maintained a spate of light social conversation, Rohan couldn't shake the idea that something was wrong, that the article had upset her way more than she was letting on. He just didn't get why.

'Are you OK?' he asked eventually as they packed up the remains of breakfast.

Her eyes widened, her smile the perfect pitch of bewilderment, her eyebrow slightly raised. 'Of course. Why wouldn't I be?'

He could let it go—should let it go. If the comments had upset Elora there was nothing he could do. He'd warned her the press would be intrusive before they had embarked on this venture. Plus he was probably imagining this. There wasn't anything in the article to upset her. She couldn't be jealous because she didn't care about him—this was a fake relationship.

And yet... 'I don't know,' he replied. 'But I know something has upset you.'

'How can you know that?'

It was a good question.

'Because you look...too calm, too unruffled. It's your frozen face. Your Ice Princess face.'

'I am a princess.'

He ignored the intervention, 'And when you read the article I saw you clench your hands. You do that when you're upset, then you pretend to be busy with something whilst you retreat behind your princess mask.'

She'd recovered herself now, the grey eyes cool and guarded.

'Of course it upset me for a moment. I'm not used to being discussed in such a way. But then I got over it. You did warn me what I was letting myself in for. I'll just need to have a thicker skin and not let it affect me.'

All very sensible words, but...

'It's not that easy,' he said. 'I know how sometimes things the press say hit a nerve and if you let those words fester they end up sticking with you, in your head. So how about you tell me what upset you and we can make sure it's in perspective?'

'Did you ever talk to anyone about the press stories about you?'

This was approaching ground he didn't want to traverse but it was a fair question.

'No, I didn't. Because I didn't have anyone I could talk to. You do. You have me. Or if you don't want to talk to me, talk to Flavia or who-ever. Because if you don't you will end up brood-ing on it. And the next article will be worse and so on. And it will end up affecting us and...'

She raised a hand. 'OK, OK, I get it. But it's not that easy. It's awkward.'

He rose to his feet. 'I've got an idea. Maybe it will be easier to talk somewhere else. Not here, surrounded by reminders of royalty. Let's go for a walk. To the local spice market. As two nor-mal people. Put on your Preeti Bannerjee clothes and I'll go incognito as well. Everyone will think we're still on the grounds—we'll be back in a couple of hours. I'll meet you by the North Door in twenty minutes.'

Twenty minutes later, they were walking along the dusty road away from the palace and Elora felt a weight lift from her, felt free in a way she only could when she shed her princess persona. Right now, no one was giving them a second glance—they were just a couple like any other amongst the busy bustle and throng of people.

Street vendors shouted their wares from the small stalls that lined the dusty road, voices were raised in the everyday barter and haggling over goods, cups of masala chai tea, potato pakoras, books, comics, a hodge-podge of offerings laid out for all to see. A few lone cattle roamed, seemingly unsupervised, people walked balancing goods upon their heads, mums holding babies cocooned to their bodies, dressed in bright saris that splashed the landscape with colour. Tourists and locals dressed in more Western clothing, young girls chattering as they walked to school.

And next to her was Rohan, dressed in casual jeans and a T-shirt, a baseball cap on his head, and a wish caught at her that they were actually a normal couple, that this wasn't yet another facet of the illusion they were conjuring.

But it was. She was a princess, an 'inexperienced, sheltered' one, a gauche woman who he was with because he had to be, and a million miles from the other women in his life. The type of women he'd chosen, and therefore she could never measure up to them.

The phrases from the article, the photos of those other women streamed through her brain and darkened the sense of lightness and in that moment she knew he was right. If she didn't talk to him about this it would affect their relationship. No, not a relationship—their agreement.

She looked up at him. 'OK, you're right. I think we should talk about the article. I'm just not sure how to start.'

'Would a cup of tea help?'

'Yes.' It would give her something to do, distract her if it got too embarrassing. 'Please.'

A few minutes later, cup of chai in hand, she tried to gather her thoughts.

'I know it was written as a frothy, gossipy article, to draw in readers, to get likes, et cetera, et cetera, but the writer had a point. I *am* an inexperienced, sheltered princess. The other women in your life weren't.' And that made her feel inadequate, small, as if she could never measure up. The way he'd looked at Caro had twisted her up inside, had made her face the fact that he had loved his first wife, whatever had happened later. And the other two women—he'd looked happy and relaxed with them, he'd chosen to be with them. Beautiful women of the world, all three of them talented celebrities in their own right. 'So how am I going to hold your attention? You chose all those other women.' She asked the question as impassively as possible, as though she were trying to pose a logical question. She wouldn't admit inadequacy to a man who clearly didn't know the meaning of the word.

'And we have chosen each other.' He looked down at her and she realised they'd slowed their steps, were attracting a few glances, and as he realised too he gestured towards the shade of a large amaltas tree, glorious with golden flowers, and a place where they could stand unnoticed. 'This isn't about "holding attention" or comparing you to other women. We have agreed to get married, to forge a marriage that is based on respect and liking and the rules and expectations we have set out. This is about you and me.'

'But we have chosen each other because of our positions. You said it yourself. Sarala is wedding Caruli. The other women in the article—you chose them because you wanted them, because you were attracted to them. Because of who they were as people. So how will we make it work long-term? How can you be faithful to someone you are marrying out of duty? How can I hold you? I'm nothing like any of those women.'

'I don't want you to be like any of them. This isn't about comparisons.' He reached out and took her empty cup from her, placed it on the ground and took her hands in his. 'Our marriage will be about you and me. I won't be comparing you to other women in my life. They are in the past. You are my future.'

'For better or worse.' She gave a laugh she recognised as brittle. 'Even that feels like a comparison.' She shook her head. 'How can I not compare myself to them? The article was right—they were all stunning, accomplished women. Experienced women. I had to watch videos on how to flirt and body language, just to prep for our date. We are faking attraction—you were really attracted to those women. We have kissed once and it was "enjoyable" and that was probably due to the novelty factor.'

She paused for breath and he jumped in.

'There's something *I* need to say.' He hesitated. 'And it's awkward for me.'

She looked up at him in patent disbelief, but saw that he meant it, there was discomfort in his expression and colour touched and heightened the planes of his cheekbones.

'Go ahead.'

'I'm not faking the attraction.' He blurted the words out. 'And that kiss. It went way beyond enjoyable. It knocked my socks off.'

He must think she was daft.

'Yet *you* described it as enjoyable,' she pointed out. 'You don't need to be kind, Rohan. I wasn't fishing for compliments.' Now her mortification was complete and she tugged her hands away.

'I am not being kind.' He dragged a hand over his face. 'I didn't say anything before because the level of attraction took me by surprise, and I don't like surprises,' he said. 'That's the honest-to-God truth. Kissing you blew me away with its intensity. The volatility made everything feel unpredictable and right now I figured we don't need that.'

Could she believe him?

'I also wasn't sure how you felt about the kiss. If you'd hated it and I'd told you the truth it would have made you uncomfortable, and that would make everything complicated.'

It made sense and she sensed that it wasn't a lie, but that didn't mean he wouldn't exaggerate to make her feel better. Yet she also heard uncertainty in his voice, as though he really didn't know how she felt about the kiss.

'I didn't hate it,' she said softly.

'And the attraction?' he asked. 'Does it exist for you or is it all faked, learnt from videos, acted for the cameras?'

She owed him truth. 'It isn't fake, but I don't understand it. As an innocent, sheltered princess, my experience of attraction is limited.' She jutted her chin out, hated the admission she was about to make. 'I've only ever kissed one other person. Once. I don't know what's normal. Plus I don't really know you. It doesn't make sense to me that I should be attracted to a man I don't know at all. And I'm not sure I like that. That kiss…it spun my head and I'm not sure I like that either.'

That kiss… The memory swirled around them now, catching her in an intoxicating net of re-membered desire. She looked at him, stand-ing there, his dark hair dappled with glints of sunshine, so vital and alive under the trailing branches, and somehow everything faded into the background—the noise, the bustle, the heat and warmth of the early morning sun washing over her, the scents and sounds of the nearby market. The heat of chillis burnished in the sun, the sweet scent of mangoes, the call of the vendors—all combining in this moment.

Sensations roiled and churned inside her, along with so many questions. How could any kiss be as magical as she remembered it? Espe-cially with a man she hardly knew, a man so far from her dream man. Was Rohan lying to her, trying to make her feel better? How could kiss-ing her, with her paucity of experience, possibly blow his mind, this man who had kissed Holly-wood royalty, the queen of the catwalk and Prin-cess Caro, a woman he'd loved?

And so… The words came, a command more than anything else.

'Kiss me again,' she said, seeing surprise touch his eyes and his expression and then un-derstanding. 'A planned kiss.' A kiss to test her memory and his word. 'Not for the cameras, not as part of a charade. A kiss between us. As people. A kiss we choose.'

'You sure?'

Of course she wasn't sure, but she was damned if she'd back down. 'I'm sure.'

He smiled at her now, a toe-curling smile that somehow also held warmth, reassurance and a promise that caught her breath.

'Don't look so worried.' The smile was in his voice too as he reached out and smoothed away the frown she hadn't even realised was there. The touch sent a shiver through her and then, oh, so gently, he ran a thumb over her lips, his skin a little hard, a little calloused, and she knew why, from the manual labour he'd put in.

The feel was exquisite and now her eyes widened as she saw his brown eyes darken and burn with desire, a desire that was for her, his gaze so intent, as though all he could see was her, truly her. Everything faded so that it was just them, nothing else mattered but this moment, and she stepped forward into his arms, looked up at him in wonder. Then he was kissing her and she was kissing him and all thoughts stopped, her whole being subsumed by the sensations that engulfed her as his lips met hers, gentle at first, teasing, tantalising, and then she was pressed against the hard length of him and he deepened the kiss in answer to her demand and she was lost.

Until finally the beep of a horn, the whiz of a bicycle going too close to them, the caw of a bird—she wasn't sure what it was, but it pulled her back to reality and she stepped back on wobbly legs, reached out to place a hand on his arm, not wanting to lose the connection, looked at him as she tried to calm her ragged breathing. He looked as shellshocked as her, desire still burned in his eyes and his breathing was as uneven as her own.

He gave a shaky laugh. 'Now do you believe me? The attraction exists.'

Her own laugh matched his. 'I think the attraction has a life of its own.'

As her heart rate slowly came down she was aware that her whole body was conflicted, a part of her glorying in the aftermath of sensation, but another part of her aware that she wanted more—more kisses, more pleasure…just more. The feelings were jagged and demanding and for once she was finding them hard to control, the iron control failing. Which was causing a sense of panic. Her ability to tame her anxieties, her fears, her emotions was part of who she was. Her hands clenched and she saw his gaze flicker to the movement and the panic increased. This man not only had caused this but he was also able to read her. In a few scant days he had upended strategies that had taken years to hone and she felt exposed, vulnerable.

'I think you were right. This is too volatile, too unpredictable, and I'm not sure either of us is comfortable with it.' The idea triggered a sense of sadness—wouldn't it be wonderful to have had this reaction to a man who wanted it, welcomed it, wanted to be with her and vice versa. A man who she could walk off with hand in hand, run to the nearest hotel and take this further, secure in love and trust.

Well, that wasn't happening and it never would. Their marriage would be an agreement, a contract where they managed expectations, but she had no idea how to manage this attraction. Her only comfort was that neither did he.

'Then let's try to keep it under wraps,' he said. 'For now. Until we get to know each other better.'

'That works.'

'But…' he gave her a smile now '…attraction is a good thing. It will be a good part of our marriage. A very good part.'

His voice sizzled with promise and it occurred to Elora that keeping attraction under wraps might not be as easy as all that. All she could think to say was, 'Let's go round the spice market.' Maybe the smells, the colours, the familiarity of the ingredients would distract her, somehow ground her.

CHAPTER TEN

ROHAN TRIED TO focus on the market—the smells, the hustle and bustle, the raucous cries of the competing sellers hawking their wares, the brightly coloured mounds of turmeric, cumin and chilli powder vibrant in their contrasting hues. But to little avail. His whole mind was filled with Elora, the simmering awareness of the woman walking next to him, an urge to throw caution to the wind, take her by the hand and book them into the nearest hotel.

Insanity.

Surely he had learnt from the mistakes of his youth, where he'd been blinded by desire for Caro, dazzled by a lust he'd never experienced before, a hostage to his hormones and libido. And all along he'd been played by Caro, a woman with way more experience, and she'd enjoyed his devotion, enjoyed making him play to her tune.

He shook his head. Elora was not like Caro—nothing like her. She wasn't deliberately manipulating him; she was just as confused as he

was. And, more to the point, he wasn't Caro—
he would not rush Elora or use this attraction
to influence her in any way. And he would not
let either of them make the mistake of mistaking lust for love. No one was getting hurt in this
marriage. Attraction would be sidelined until
they had everything else in place. Because he
could sense how troubled she was, knew that he
was the cause of that trouble. That something
that should be good and positive was becoming
complicated.

'Elora?'

'Yes.'

'Are you feeling any better about the article?'

'I'm not sure,' she admitted. 'I'm glad that
the attraction exists and is mutual but…it also
seems to have complicated things. And it still
doesn't really solve the problem. We haven't chosen each other. How can you help but compare
me to them?'

'I won't. I don't want to, any more than you can
compare these vegetables.' He gestured towards
the wicker baskets heaped with firm red tomatoes,
bunches of long, thin green chillis, dark green
okra and the bitter gourd. 'This one is bitter, this
one is hot, this one is long, another is short.'

'I don't think your analogy holds. People don't
only eat one vegetable—they enjoy a variety.

Because one day you may want bitter, another sweet.'

'And you can get that from one particular vegetable,' he said. 'You can use chillies to make something hot and spicy that blows your mind, another day you could deseed it and have something gentler, another day you could make a sweet chilli sauce or... And you can be faithful to one seller of all vegetables.'

Now she stared at him and he shook his head. 'OK. You're right—this is a terrible analogy. What else can I do to try and help, apart from promise you I would never compare you to anyone else, because you are unique? You are you.'

But he could see his words still weren't helping.

'I'm not sure. I think...part of the problem is that I have no knowledge of relationships; I've never had one. So, even if I want to, I have nothing to compare you to, so I don't know if I can believe you.'

The words were simple and yet they hit him like a sucker punch on the back of his previous thoughts. When he'd met Caro he'd never had a relationship, had mistaken lust for love. He'd got married expecting the whole happy ever, hadn't had a clue how to manage his feelings or accept he'd got it wrong. Had tormented himself with jealousy over her previous relationships, had been a mess.

'Can you tell me something about yours—not your marriage, I understand that's off-limits—but perhaps the two other women in the article? I'm trying to figure out how we can work when I'm so different to the type of women you choose to be with.'

'What do you want to know?'

She shrugged. 'I'm not sure. How did you meet? What went wrong?'

'I met them both at parties. I met Charlotte at a premiere of one of her films. She approached me, we got talking and ended up having dinner the next day. It was a very straightforward relationship. She had never dated a prince, she said it was on her to-do list. We got on, we liked each other, both of us knew it wasn't serious. We went out for a bit, did a few interviews where I promoted Sarala and she promoted her film. Then, when she landed her next starring role, we decided it was time to go our separate ways. Completely amicably, no drama, no fuss.

'It was much the same with Marianne—we met at a party, got on, decided to have some fun. She decided to end it a few months ago, when the unrest first broke out on Baluka—we had a conversation about possible outcomes. She decided it was best to call it a day. I think she had

hopes of becoming a princess, but once she realised that could lead to becoming a deposed
princess she bailed.'

'Did you mind?'

'Not in the slightest,' he said truthfully. 'I'd
always been clear that marriage wasn't on the
cards. I did choose to be with them, Elora, but
I never saw them in my long-term future. They
were casual relationships.'

She nodded, a small frown on her forehead.
'Did you ever love them?'

'No. I liked them. I enjoyed their company
and I don't regret my time with them, but love
was never in the mix.'

'So it was like a temporary contract. A different agreement to ours, with a different rulebook.
But essentially the same idea.'

'Perhaps. But the idea behind our marriage is
permanence.'

'So the poll is flawed. I will hold you because
I am the Princess of Caruli.'

'I can't change the fact that we are marrying
for political reasons, but I can say that I truly believe that what we are creating now will give us
a bedrock, the foundation to a successful marriage.'

'But you didn't manage that with Caro.'

'No, I didn't. But you aren't Caro and I have
learnt from my mistakes.' He pressed his lips

together, grateful that Elora didn't push it, even more grateful and a little bit surprised when a minute later he felt her hand slip into his as they continued to walk round the market.

'I'd like to buy some things to give to your parents,' she said. 'Just everyday things from the market, or maybe I could buy some ingredients and cook something for them?'

Without even meaning to, he squeezed her hand, grateful for the change of topic. It was as though she not only respected but understood that he didn't want to relive the bad memories.

'That's a good idea,' he said.

And as they walked and looked at the stalls and discussed what she could make, as they walked back to the palace holding a bag of food, he wished that they really could be Preeti Bannerjee and Rohan Carmody. But they weren't and later today he would return to Sarala, to the island he was destined to rule, however little he wished for that destiny.

Once back at the palace they slipped inside and Elora glanced at her watch. 'We're late. We'd better hurry. My mother disapproves of unpunctuality.'

Rohan nodded and within ten minutes they were both back downstairs and at the door of the reception room. No wonder no one recognised Preeti and Elora as being one and the same. Elora looked a million miles from the woman he'd walked hand in hand with, and yet when she'd met his gaze he'd seen a glimmer of his Elora.

Whoa. His? Stop right there.

Elora wasn't his.

'We'd better go in,' she said, and there was a hint of trepidation in her voice.

They entered, to be met by a disapproving look, aimed at Elora. 'You're late.'

'I apologise, Mama. I was preparing for the journey to Sarala.'

'That is no excuse. A princess shows respect through punctuality. I expect you to remember that.'

'Yes, Mama.'

Rohan opened his mouth to at least take some of the blame, but, before he could, Elora gave her head the smallest shake and he knew it was a signal to let it be.

The door opened and the equerry announced Flavia and Viraj, who, Rohan noted, were not reprimanded for their lateness.

'Hello, Viraj. I've been looking forward to seeing you,' Rohan said and the little boy beamed, just as the Queen spoke.

'There has been a slight change of plan. Viraj, you will understand. I have agreed to a meeting with a local pro-royalist group; it is a good publicity opportunity and a chance to remind the people there is continuity.'

Rohan glanced at the little boy, saw the beam fade to disappointment and then resignation, saw Elora look at her sister, then her mother, and open her mouth as if to protest, saw the look the Queen gave her, so cold that Rohan instinctively stepped forward.

'Actually,' he said, 'I don't think that will work.'

The Queen's grey eyes glittered, but courtesy dictated a civil answer. 'Viraj understands that duty comes before pleasure—there will be other times…'

'Not like today,' Rohan said firmly. 'I know and I appreciate your daughters' and your grandson's desire to do their duty, but I also believe that sometimes, where possible, it is acceptable to make sure pleasure is part of life and that makes the duty more pleasurable. I made a promise to Viraj and a prince always keeps his promises. Or at least this one does.'

Flavia stepped forward. 'Perhaps Viraj could spend some time with Rohan and Elora, so the Prince can keep his promise, and I will speak with the delegation, and then we could carry out a photo opportunity.'

'That way, pleasure and duty are covered.'

Viraj entered the fray. 'Please. I promise I will

do everything right for the photos and I will do extra studies as well.'

Rohan said nothing else, but he admired Viraj's intervention, giving the Queen a reason to relent under the guise of being a doting grandmother, without losing face.

'Very well.' The words were snapped but they were an acquiescence. 'Elora, make sure you take good care of Viraj.'

'Of course, Mama.' Elora's voice was even but he could sense the tension, saw her put a hand behind her back, knew she was clenching it. Though by the time they left the room she was smiling down at Viraj. 'Ready to make cake?'

'Yes, please.'

'You can be chief chef,' Rohan offered.

'Yes, Your Highness.'

'You can call me Rohan.'

'Are you sure? Grandmama says…'

'Well, Grandmama isn't here. And I am giving you permission to call me Rohan.'

The little boy nodded. 'My tutor says I must make a good impression,' he explained. 'Because one day you will rule Sarala and I will rule Caruli. So it is important you see that I am strong and sensible.'

'Perhaps it is more important to make sure that we are friends,' he suggested, wishing with all

his heart that this little boy could be just that—
a little boy. 'And to have fun.'

Viraj looked unconvinced. 'But if I have fun,
how will you take me seriously?'

'I promise I will take you seriously, but we can
have fun as well. All of us together.'

They had reached the kitchens now. 'OK,'
Elora said. 'Aprons on and let's get started.'

Rohan watched how carefully Elora listened
to Viraj's questions. Instead of telling him what
to do, she helped him read the recipe, figure it
out and let him do everything, his tongue poking
out in concentration as he measured the flour.

'I got it wrong.'

'Hey. That's OK.'

'But it's not. Princes can't get things wrong.'

'Yes, they can,' Rohan said. 'Because sometimes that's how they learn. If you don't get things
wrong, how will you ever learn to get them right?
The important thing is to learn from your mistakes and not beat yourself up about them.'

'Is that what you do?'

'It's what I try to do. So just have another go at
the measuring and this time I'm sure you'll get it
right. But if you don't you can have another go.'

Half an hour later, the cake was in the oven.

'Now for the best bit,' Rohan said. 'We scrape
the bowl and eat the cake mix.'

He waited for Viraj to swoop on the bowl.

Instead, the little boy turned a worried face to him. 'I think it would make me ill. That's what Grandmama says. She told Mummy off when I ate some raw cookie dough and…'

'Then maybe it's best if we don't,' Elora said quickly. 'We can eat the cake instead when it's ready.'

Rohan glanced at Elora and saw that her expression mirrored Viraj's, a mask of worry.

'OK. New plan for the cake mix.' He was making this up as he went along now. 'We'll use it to make a diplomatic pact of friendship. Everyone grab a spoon.' Dammit, he was going to make Viraj and Elora have at least a little bit of fun. He handed out the spoons. 'Hold your spoon up and repeat after me. We vow to be friends.'

Elora gave a sudden smile and nodded at Viraj, who held his spoon up and repeated the words.

'And now,' Rohan said, 'to seal the pact.' And, quick as a flash, he'd scooped up a bit of cake mix and dabbed it on Elora's nose and then on Viraj's. 'Now, you do the same.'

And suddenly Viraj was giggling as he dabbed the blobs of cake mix and Elora's low chuckle joined in. Then somehow Rohan dipped his fingers in the flour and swiped at Elora's cheek and everyone was laughing as Elora chased Viraj across the kitchen, and they were so immersed they didn't notice the door swing open until a voice rang out, 'Announcing Her Majesty Queen Joanna.'

Rohan saw Elora freeze for an instant before swiftly stepping in front of Viraj, who instantly raised a hand to his face to wipe away the evidence.

'What is going on here?'

'Nothing, Mama. We have made the cake.'

'And now you are running around like fools,' the Queen said. 'On a slippery floor, where Viraj could slip, fall, get injured. Is this how you take care of the heir to Caruli? Is this what you teach him? To make mess, be disorderly?'

'Grandmama, it is not Elora's fault.' Viraj stepped out from behind Elora.

'Yes, Viraj, it is. I foolishly entrusted you to her. Now go—you need to prepare.'

'But…'

'It's OK, Viraj. Go,' Elora said. 'I will see you later.'

The Queen waited until Viraj left and turned back to Elora. 'I am disappointed, Elora.'

'I am sorry, Mama.'

Rohan knew he needed to say something. He had been so taken aback by the Queen's over-reaction that he'd stayed silent.

'Actually,' he began, 'this isn't all down to Elora and Viraj was just having a bit of fun.'

The Queen turned to Rohan and managed a

wintry smile. 'I appreciate your intervention, Rohan, and I will take your words on board. However, we do things differently here on Caruli and it is important that everyone understands how Viraj is to be treated. Elora does know. I will speak with her on your return from Sarala.'

Rohan opened his mouth and then saw that Elora had turned her gaze on him, a plea in her grey eyes, and he knew she wanted him to say no more, even if it were in her defence.

'Yes, Mama,' she said.

'Now, please go to the stables and prepare.'

'The stables?'

'Yes. You are all going to ride in procession to the ferry. The people always love a horseback procession. Please don't be late.'

'Um…perhaps I should stay here, clear up the kitchen and I could…'

The Queen's expression of exasperation caused Elora to break off.

'I have told you what needs to be done. Do it. The cake is not important. Switch the oven off and I will ask someone to come and sort out the mess in here.'

Rohan clenched his teeth together, wanted to throw all traditional respect for his elders out of the window seeing the pallor of Elora's face.

He waited until the Queen swept out and turned to Elora, who raised a hand. 'It's OK, Rohan.

Please leave it. I need to go and get ready. I'll meet you at the stables.'

Without another look at him, she left the room.

Elora studied her face in the mirror, made sure every trace of flour had gone, that the mask of make-up she'd applied hid her pallor. At least now her hands were no longer shaking, at least she'd made it out of the kitchen and to her room before the panic had hit, before the onset of the shallow breathing, the pounding of her heart, the beat and throb of fear in her chest and at her temples.

It had been the shock of it. Usually, she had warning of when she would be in the proximity of a horse, advance notice that she would be required to ride. But today it had been sprung on her, with no chance to do her usual preparations. But she'd have to manage, could only imagine her mother's wrath if Elora collapsed in an undignified heap. And Rohan—she didn't want Rohan to know about this, didn't even want to acknowledge it herself. For a moment the image of Sanjay on that last day threatened and she pushed it down—couldn't afford to let that memory in now or she wouldn't be able to enter the stables, let alone ride.

One more swig of her herbal remedy against panic, two more minutes of deep breathing and then she touched the talisman she carried everywhere with her. Sanjay's ring—a beaded ring they'd made together as children.

Now she was ready. As she headed down to the stables she was entirely focused on her breathing, on projecting an aura of calm, knowing the horses would sense even the slightest hint of nerves. But she managed a smile for Viraj, safely ensconced on a horse with a groom behind him, ensuring his safety.

Rohan stepped towards her and she saw the questions in his dark eyes, relieved that at least he would ascribe any tension to the encounter with her mother. 'You OK?' he asked, and the warmth in his voice warmed her.

'I'm good,' she said as a groom brought her horse towards her, and she saw with relief that it was Jaswant, the one person who knew the depths of her fear of horses, the one person who had shown her sympathy, helped her to manage over the years. Without him, she had no idea how she would or could have coped.

He helped her onto the horse, kept a soothing hand on the thoroughbred until the last moment. 'He'll be good,' he said briefly, the words he used every time, words that held a promise that Elora believed.

She waited as three members of the pro-royalist group were also helped onto horses from the stables, saw their excited faces, as photos were taken, managed to play her part and smile, grateful that Jaswant was still standing nearby.

And then they were off and all she focused on was getting through the ordeal. She told herself the journey was at least short, and a glance at Rohan showed her that he rode with an assurance and confidence that meant he should be safe. Viraj too would be OK, held firmly in place by one of the palace's most experienced grooms. And she was flanked by them, so the crowds weren't focused on her.

But, in some ways, perhaps that made it worse because now, as she saw the crowds cheer Viraj, captivated by his youth and the knowledge that they beheld their future ruler, knowing she wasn't being watched made it harder for Elora to keep her smile in place.

Now, all she was aware of was the immensity of the horse beneath her, the power of the creature's muscles, the height from the ground and the horrible knowledge of how easily everything could go wrong in a heartbeat. And with that treacherous thought came a sudden flashback to that awful day…the smell of the horses, her own terror, the realisation that she was going to fail, that she would not be able to keep her fear of horses in check. And then Sanjay, wanting to help her…and in the process, in a scant few minutes, tragedy had struck.

Oh, God. She felt herself sway in the saddle, was suddenly aware of an outstretched hand— Rohan's. Strong, safe, secure, and it galvanised her. This time she would not cause further tragedy. Straightening, she put her smile back in place and somehow made it through the rest of the journey to the ferry port.

And only now did she really think about her destination, recall that now she and Rohan were taking their charade, their illusion, to Sarala, an island where there was more unrest, an island where Prince Rohan was regarded with suspicion, and new anxiety rippled through her.

CHAPTER ELEVEN

As the ferry approached Sarala, Rohan stood next to Elora and regarded the looming coastline, the familiar curve of sandy beach, the angles of the tree-lined hills.

He loved his country and yet, the nearer they came, he felt a heaviness in his chest, a heaviness caused by the sure knowledge that he didn't want or deserve the destiny his birth had conferred on him, that he was not cut out to rule this land, though he would do his very best. He'd always known it, but he'd accepted his fate as inescapable. That acceptance was harder now that he'd found something he did want to do. But there was no hope of that; this he knew deep down, though he would try his best to persuade his parents that he could take on a dual role—run his business and fulfil his duties as heir.

He looked down at Elora, standing next to him, tendrils of blonde hair rippling in the sea breeze. There had been no opportunity to speak on the journey, the hour taken up in the charade, speaking to fellow passengers, posing for photographs, all of which Elora had done with grace and poise and friendliness. Despite the fact he knew she'd withdrawn, and how could he blame her after that scene in the kitchen? He wanted to speak to her about it, but he was waiting for a chance to get her in private.

But first there would be the arrival party, the greetings with his family and then... 'Later today,' he said, 'I plan on visiting a temple—an old temple on Sarala, a place I always go to when I get home. Would you like to come? It isn't part of the publicity—no press, no photos.'

'Yes, I would. As long as I won't be intruding.'

'You won't. I'd like to show it to you.'

The words were nothing more than the truth; it was a place where he found peace and perhaps Elora would too.

'But first we need to get through the fanfare of our arrival.'

And it was indeed a fanfare, as they left the ferry with a smile and a wave to the people waiting, walked towards the car that would take them to the palace.

The press was out in force and one of the reporters threw a question. 'Princess Elora, how was your first date? And Prince Rohan, how does Elora measure up?'

He tensed and next to him he felt Elora's nails

pinch his arm in warning, as she stopped and turned.

'It is very early days and right now our priority is to show each other our islands. We will be doing a number of state events together, because we are hoping to show our people that we are here and hoping they will put their faith in us as the future. And we are here to listen. And...' she raised a hand '...I know that didn't answer your question. As first dates go, it was...pretty good and you'll be glad to know that His Highness measured up to *my* expectations. Other than that, a princess doesn't kiss and tell.'

Rohan knew it was time to say his piece. 'All I can say is that if the Princess agrees, I am hoping whilst she is here to take her on date number two and three and four. As for measuring up, Elora is in a field of her own and I would never presume to compare her to anyone, and I'd appreciate it if none of you did either.'

It was the best that he could do and even that wasn't easy, given what he wanted to do was take the reporter and kick him into the sea. But, instead, they continued their walk to the waiting car and then smiled and waved their way to the palace.

There on the steps were his parents and Marisa, waiting to greet them. Marisa stepped forward.

'Welcome, little bro and Elora, it's lovely to see you again.'

'Indeed.' Queen Kaamini stepped forward and took Elora's hands in hers. 'Welcome, Elora. The King and I look forward to getting to know you better over the next days. We also have a number of events planned.'

'Amma! Give Elora a chance to get her bearings,' Rohan said.

'No, Rohan. It's fine. I like to have as much preparation time as possible. I would be happy to discuss the agenda for my visit.'

'But first I will show Elora to her room. I have put you next door to me. I hope that is all right.'

'That sounds wonderful.'

'It does,' Rohan said. 'Now, though, I am taking Elora to the temple.'

His sister's gaze flicked to him and he saw the hint of surprise that he was taking Elora to a place that usually only he and she now visited. He had never even taken Caro there. But he knew if they didn't go now, they would get swallowed up in royal duties and he would never have the chance to find out what was going on.

'We will be back in a couple of hours and then we are all yours,' he said.

'I will hold you to that,' the King said. 'There are matters to discuss.'

Rohan bowed his head, then gestured to Elora.

'Where is the temple?' she asked as they left the palace and headed towards the car port that housed the royal fleet of cars.

'Not far. It is on the palace grounds, but if we are to be back in time it will be better to drive.'

After ten minutes he parked by the side of the road near some woodlands. 'We can walk from here.'

As they headed through the woods the air was scented with the evergreen smell of the trees that provided a welcome shade from the heat of the sun. They walked in a silence broken only by the sound of birds, the metallic note of the coppersmith, the tap of a woodpecker and the chatter of the parakeets.

She looked at him. 'Your family were so welcoming. I appreciate that.'

'They are relieved that our marriage is going ahead, relieved that we are here. As long as Sarala is served, my parents will always be gracious.' He replayed the words and then shook his head. 'That was discourteous of me. My parents are good, kind people who I love and who love me. But what you do need to understand about them, now you are being welcomed into the family, is that however much they love me, however much they love Marisa, they love Sarala more.

And they would admit that freely—they see no wrong in it.'

'But at least they show grace and love,' Elora said.

They reached the temple now and she slowed. 'Oh, I didn't realise it would be so…old. It feels awe-inspiring, like stepping back in history.'

'It was built back in the tenth century. At some point a ruler let it fall into disrepair, perhaps when war and fighting meant there was no money, and in recent times it has been difficult to justify spending money on a temple that is on private palace grounds.'

'Yet it still holds such beauty,' she said softly as they both looked at the remains of what once must have been a vast edifice. But Elora was right—what was left was still a thing of beauty. Stone steps led up to a rectangular base, with beautifully carved stone pillars that rose majestically to support a now moss-laden domed roof.

'I come here to think. It's a place my grandfather used to bring me to. He didn't have a lot of free time, but when he did he'd come here with me. I think its age puts things into perspective, makes me feel part of a whole pattern, part of Sarala and all its traditions and the history it is steeped in.'

'History both good and bad,' she said. 'History that is in the making right now, and not only for us, for royalty, but for every single inhabitant on this island. Centuries ago, we fought and battled for our independence from each other, to prevent our ancestors from taking our lands and seas. Now, Baluka has battled for its republic, for democracy. And people died, not soldiers on the battlefield, but people caught up in history, people in the wrong place at the wrong time—one person got caught in a wave of protests and was trampled underfoot.' Her voice broke. 'When I think about that, that person and their family, it all seems so unfair. Yet some would say there is always a price to pay. For freedom.'

'Or to keep power,' he said.

'But that's not what it's about, is it?' she asked. 'I don't think our parents want power. I know I don't. I think they just believe in their divine right to rule and they believe they are blessed to be given it.'

'And in return they give their all to ruling, do their best to be just and bring good to the people and the land. And they would sacrifice anything to do that,' Rohan said.

'And I suppose that's why your parents love you but love Sarala more.'

'And why your parents guard Viraj so carefully.' He hesitated. 'I want to apologise for earlier. When I suggested he had fun, encouraged the food fight, I didn't mean to bring down your mother's anger on your head.'

'It's OK.'

'But I wish you had let me explain—and, more than that, to perhaps make your mother see that what we did wasn't wrong. That poor child was only having a little bit of fun. My parents let me have some fun. If I had said something...'

'It would have made no difference,' Elora said with a weariness in her voice that touched his heart. 'Could even have made things worse. If you had defended me, my mother would be more likely to veto any further suggestions we spend time with him. Viraj would suffer.'

'So in future I have to stand back and allow your mother to say whatever she likes to you? I'm not sure I can do that.' He hesitated. 'I don't know Queen Joanna or the ins and outs of your relationship, but sometimes when people are naturally autocratic it is better to stand up to them, rather than just accept it. I know that is difficult in our culture, where respect for our elders is so important, but perhaps your mother isn't even aware of what she is doing. Next time, maybe it will *help* if I speak to her...'

'No!' Now Elora's voice was sharp and, realising it, she lifted a hand. 'I know you want to help, but truly it will be better to leave it. Anyway, hopefully, after our marriage my mother will change, but if she doesn't it's OK. I don't mind.'

He looked at her, wondered how she could not mind. 'I may need more than that. I am not sure I will always be able to hold my tongue. You will be my wife—how can I stand by and not defend you?'

The question appeared to catch her by surprise. 'We can make it part of our agreement,' she said steadily. 'That you are allowed to stand by, that that is my expectation of you.'

'Then you will need to explain. I cannot agree to a term I disagree with and don't understand.'

She sighed now. 'My mother has never got over Sanjay's death. I'm not sure that she ever will—either of my parents. Sanjay was their... hope for the future, their pride, their joy. Their world, I suppose you could say.'

'And he was your brother, your twin. I cannot imagine the pain of your loss.'

'No,' she said simply. 'I don't think anyone can unless they have experienced it. But for my parents it wasn't only the loss of a child. It was the loss of the heir. Made worse by the fact my mother didn't fall pregnant again. She was forty when Sanjay died and she still hoped for years that it would happen, but it didn't, and because of that she slowly became more and more bitter and despairing. And afraid.'

'Afraid of what?' The penny dropped before she had answered. 'She was scared your father would divorce her and remarry.'

'Yes. After all, he'd already done it once. He divorced Flavia's mother because after Flavia she had a number of miscarriages. He met my mother whilst he was abroad and what started as an affair became serious and he decided to marry her. Decided that it was worth the risk of a public backlash, gambled that the people would forgive him once an heir was born.'

'That must have affected Flavia very much.'

'It must have, but she has never spoken to me about it. She went abroad to live with her mother. She only came back when Sanjay died. Because that was her duty.'

'To return and marry and produce an heir,' Rohan said.

'Like you. And once she had Viraj my mother's position was more assured. But I don't believe either of my parents, especially my mother, will ever get over Sanjay's death. And I'm his twin, the one who is still here, I am a constant reminder to them of that loss. They lost him and they were left with me, and they wouldn't have been human if they hadn't wished it had been me who died. My father can hardly bear to look at me—when he does, it is with such sadness, such weariness I could weep. My mother shows her feelings through anger because every time she sees me it causes her pain and grief.'

His heart tore at her words—words he wanted to refute and deny but he knew he couldn't. He'd seen how her parents were around her, couldn't even put his hand on his heart and say that his parents wouldn't be a little the same. But he knew too that, however much they grieved, they would never treat their remaining daughter with cruelty, would never stop loving her.

'They are wrong,' he said flatly. 'To grieve the loss of a son, the loss of an heir, is understandable, and I feel for them, but to treat you badly… that is wrong. This is all wrong.'

'Perhaps, but it is as it is. That too is part of our tradition. I am sure in centuries past so many kings and queens cursed and rued the day a daughter was born instead of a longed-for son.' She shook her head. 'I don't want sympathy. I am just trying to explain why I don't wish you to challenge my mother or stand up for me. Nothing can change how she feels about me, but if telling me what to do, belittling me, gives her any comfort then let her have it.'

He frowned, and wondered why she was so accepting of her mother's attitude. It was almost as though she felt she deserved it, and yet that made no sense.

'It still is wrong. If we have daughters, I swear

to you, here in this holy place, that I will love them. I will love them for being the individual human beings they are, I will love them because they are my child, part of me, and I will never curse, regret or rue that they are a girl. I need you to believe this. To trust me on this if you can't trust me on anything else.'

He saw confusion in her eyes and then the sparkle of tears as her lips parted.

'I…' Then she looked away for a moment and back at him. 'I do believe you.'

He frowned, sure that she'd meant to say something else, and then she rose to her feet and repeated the words. 'I do believe you. Thank you. And I will do everything to make this marriage work.' And, reaching up, she kissed his cheek, the touch so gentle, so sweet, he thought he felt his heart ache.

They stood hand in hand for a long moment and then, as if to break the spell, she stepped back and glanced at her watch.

'We'd better get back.'

He nodded agreement and with one last backward glance they headed to the car.

CHAPTER TWELVE

ONCE BACK AT the palace they were pulled into an instant whirlwind of activity. First, they had a meeting with both King and Queen to outline the events planned for the next days, complete with allocated time slots left for 'romance'.

'We thought we'd leave that bit to you,' the Queen explained, 'but if you need any props or organisational help let us know.'

'I think we'll manage,' Rohan said quickly, and Elora smiled, taking it all in. His family were so different from her own, their conversations easy and courteous, with a teasing tone that would be unimaginable in her own home.

Then, once the meeting was done, Marisa entered the room. 'I'll take you to your room,' she said.

Elora followed Marisa through a palace that was in many ways like her own home in Caruli, marble-floored, portraits on the wall and a massive oak staircase sweeping to the second floor.

'Here you are.' Marisa pushed the door open

to a spacious suite of rooms, her suitcase already placed on the king-sized bed.

'Thank you.'

'It is we who should be thanking you. Not every princess would agree to take on my brother. I understand it's a tall order, and I assure you Rohan is a good man. But we are grateful—Sarala needs this marriage and a marriage that strengthens an alliance with a neighbour in these times is welcome. Now all we need is an heir.'

The words sent that familiar shiver of anxiety through her, an anxiety already triggered by the conversation with Rohan by the temple. Because that had shown more than a desire for an heir—there had spoken a man who wanted a family, be they sons or daughters. And she'd been so close to sharing her fears with him, telling him the truth about the possibility of fertility issues, but in the end she couldn't take that risk.

'I understand,' Elora said. 'I understand too that it is important to make the people believe that Rohan is a good man. With the times as unstable as they are, they need an heir they trust to rule well.'

'Yes.' For the first time in the conversation Marisa glanced away, her gaze fixed on the window, looking out towards the capital city. Elora wondered for a moment how Marisa felt about the law that meant she could not rule simply because she was a female, despite the fact she was the elder. 'We are hoping that this romance idea will help with that, show him in a softer light. But I should warn you that it will not be easy. Here on Sarala, there are more republican sympathisers—there is more poverty here—but also there is animosity towards Rohan, an animosity my brother has done little to allay.'

Because he was guilty? The idea that she had been so sure of just days ago no longer seemed so easy to believe. How could the man who had kissed her, held her, and promised to love daughters as much as sons, be the ruthless prince portrayed by the press? The husband who had terrorised his wife into flight.

Yet it had happened—the foiled escape, the divorce—and never once had Rohan given his side of the story. Did Marisa know the truth? It was a question Elora wouldn't ask. If Rohan did not wish to share the facts with her then she would not go behind his back to discover them. Nor would she ask Marisa to betray her brother's confidence, even assuming he had confided in her. Probably not, given Caro had once been, maybe still even was, a friend of Marisa.

'If the animosity is deep-seated it will be difficult to shift.'

'Yes, but at least my parents are well liked. I doubt the people would move against them, but it is the future we must protect. Caro was a popular princess, which means you will have to work extra hard to win their liking. The best way to do this is to have an heir.'

That word again, and she had to deflect the subject.

'That takes time. In the short-term, what would you advise?'

'Be as natural as possible. If you believe in Rohan, people will see that and they will take that seriously. Play the romance card, but don't overdo it. Make it all as believable as you can. As you know, Caro was my friend, but that doesn't blind me to her faults. She and Rohan were always ill-suited. Caro likes drama and she likes being at the centre of it and, as a born actress, she is an expert at creating drama and illusions. I suggest you skip the drama and create better illusions. And get Rohan on board. He can't stand the press; you'll need to keep him on track. I'll help as much as I can.' Marisa smiled. 'But now I'll leave you, give you a bit of a chance to process things before dinner. And good luck.'

Elora had the feeling she'd need it.

But over the next days her luck held. She and Rohan attended the events organised by his parents, charity galas and walkabouts, visits to factories, and in between they fitted in a couple of 'dates', a dinner at a small local restaurant and a trip to a theatre to watch a performance by a local playwright. Both venues had been suggested by Marisa and both felt very public— Elora and Rohan on show as they chatted to fellow diners and theatregoers. Press coverage was neither enthusiastic nor vitriolic; Elora had a sense of suspended judgement.

On the fourth morning of her visit she entered the breakfast room, once again enjoying the fact that here on Sarala there was less pomp and ceremony, no need to be announced. But she sensed a very different atmosphere to what she was used to here, the tension evident—Rohan's expression stiff and grim, his parents' resolute. The Queen dabbed at her mouth with a napkin.

'So what are the plans for today?' Elora asked, needing to say something. 'I see we have romance slotted in.'

'*I've* planned a picnic,' Rohan said, managing a smile. 'I thought we were due a date where we aren't on show.'

'However, I have arranged for a horse and carriage to take you to your destination,' the King said. 'With Carulian horses, descendants of a gift from your grandfather to my father.'

It took all her years of training, all her experience of controlling anxiety to allow her to smile.

'Thank you. It will feel like another sign of the alliance between our countries.'

'You'll also be able to assess how many pro-testers line the streets and how many supporters,' Marisa said. 'Far easier in a carriage than a car.'

'There will also be plenty of security present.'

'Undercover, presumably?' Marisa said and the King nodded.

'A judicious mix. Enough that people are aware of them but not so many that it causes undue comment.'

'Where are we going?' Elora tried to sound ca-sual, wanting to assess the length of the journey, and told herself it would be fine even without the familiar turbaned figure of Jaswant behind the horses. She would be in a carriage; it wasn't as though she had to ride a horse.

She saw Rohan's dark eyes rest on her thought-fully, and then he answered. 'We're going to a royal nature park. Private land. And beautiful. About half an hour away.'

The words were said in his usual deep rumble, but she could still sense the tension in the room. Knew something had been said before her ar-rival at the breakfast table. She ate deliberately slowly, waited until the King, Queen and Marisa had exited the room and then turned to Rohan.

'What happened?'

At first, she thought he wouldn't answer. Then

he shrugged. 'I told my parents about my business and, in brief, they have instructed me to close it down or hand it over to someone else.' His voice was matter-of-fact, but she knew how much it would hurt, recalled the enthusiasm, the vitality he'd shown when he told her about the hotel. Knew how much of himself he'd invested in the business.

'What if you moved it to Sarala?' she asked. 'What if you built up tourism, resorts on Sarala?'

'I suggested that and Marisa backed that as a positive idea. That was when they said I should hand the business over to someone who "will have the time and energy to invest in it to maximise the benefit to Sarala" and that person cannot be me as I will need to put my all into preparing to rule and then actually ruling Sarala. That I must do my duty.' He cradled his coffee cup. 'Duty comes first.'

The unfairness of it all tore at her. Rohan was willing to do his duty, to rule, to give up so much. To marry a woman he didn't want to marry, to move back here.

'Are you sure they won't change their minds?'

'I'm sure. They believe I need to focus exclusively on Sarala.'

'But your business was for Sarala.' She frowned. 'What if you start the business up now, whilst you

are the heir? What if I offer to help? I can learn—
if there are two of us, then...'

He looked at her and now his smile was genuine, warmed his dark eyes. 'Would you do that?
For me? That isn't in our agreement.'

'No, it isn't. But yes, I would do that, because
I know how much your dream means to you and
I would like you to be able to fulfil at least a part
of that dream.'

'It's a kind thought, but I know my parents.
They will not change their minds and I will not
complain. Now, we had better make ready for
the procession. The picnic at the end will be
worth it.'

The finality in his tone indicated that the subject was closed and now...now she needed to
prepare. Make sure she did her duty and didn't
make a fool of herself.

Rohan helped Elora up into the carriage, aware
that she seemed a little more tense than she had
been on previous public outings on Sarala. Perhaps it was simply the whole waving and smiling
gig. He'd been touched at her reaction earlier;
it had felt good to know she truly got what it
meant to him, but also understood that he had
no choice. His destiny was unavoidable. As now
was hers. His to rule, hers to marry him and
carry an heir.

Once seated, he saw her flick a quick glance forward and he introduced her to the carriage driver. 'This is Deepak; he has been working in the stables for ten years and he loves these horses.'

Then he concentrated on the crowds that lined the streets, observed the number of pro-republican placards amongst those who had simply come to watch their progress. But the protestors were peaceful enough, and Rohan was waving on automatic, his brain still conjuring ways to try to change his parents' minds, even though he knew it was a futile endeavour.

They were about halfway on their journey when he became aware that a group of protest-ers had started a chant and then everything hap-pened all at once. A shout, the whinny of a horse as it startled, the whirr of an object lobbed from the crowd…a scream from Elora

Without thought, he had an arm around her and pulled her down. She must have been hit—the cry had been so full of fear. What the hell had been thrown? White-hot anger and panic converged inside him.

'Where are you hurt?'

The groom had the horses under control now, but the crowds were jostling with noise and excla-mation and security was about to surround them.

She sat up, pushed his hand away. 'I'm fine.' She twisted in her seat. 'We have to go back.'

'Go back. Why?'

'Please…' Her voice broke. 'Please trust me. We have to go back.'

A moment's thought and then, 'Turn round,' he ordered.

'But Your Highness…'

'You heard me.'

'But…' Now it was the security officer. 'I am sorry, Your Highness, but…'

'Rohan—' Elora's voice was urgent '—please.'

'I said turn around. This is my call, my responsibility and, believe me, I will be listened to. Do it now.'

Security pulled away as the groom turned the carriage.

'Where do you want to go?'

'Back to where it happened. We have to stop Security from getting involved. I am not hurt. Nothing happened. This is my fault.'

In minutes they were back and instantly she scrambled down. He jumped down after her, beckoned to Security, who helped push through until they found the protesters circled by a ring of security officers.

'Please stand down.' Elora's voice was clear and incisive. 'I'm not hurt and I'm not pressing any charges. You can leave. I wish to speak to these people.' Elora was every inch a princess now, but she wasn't in her own country and Rohan stepped up next to her.

'Listen to the Princess. But stay within calling distance. And keep everyone else away.'

Once they had backed off, he turned back to Elora. 'Now what?'

'Now we talk to them,' she said. She was calmer now as she looked at the group of four, aged between eighteen and twenty-three at a guess, two boys, two girls.

'Are any of you hurt?'

'No. Why? Did you expect your security to hurt us?'

'No,' Elora said. 'But I understand how sometimes people can get carried away. If Security believed I had been hurt then it is possible they could have been overzealous. I just wanted to be sure.'

'Given you threw something at the Princess and could have injured her or caused an accident, I am not sure you should be so belligerent,' Rohan said. 'If my groom had lost control of the carriage there could have been a lot worse damage.'

'What did you throw?' Elora asked.

'A tomato,' one of the girls admitted. 'It wasn't planned. It was part of my lunch. It was in my hand and I heard the chanting and I saw the placards and I thought that I needed to do something and then, almost before I knew it, I'd thrown it.'

'A tomato is hardly a deadly weapon,' one of the boys said.

'My security forces weren't to know that,' Rohan pointed out. 'I wasn't to know that. The people here weren't to know that.'

'Also, it was a terrible throw,' another protester said. 'I didn't think it could possibly have hit you.'

'It didn't.'

Rohan glanced at her; he'd been sure she'd been hurt, but events had all happened so fast.

'But that wouldn't have mattered,' Elora said softly. 'Just by throwing that tomato, you could have caused a real accident. Security were surrounding you—it could have triggered further protest, violent protest, people could have got hurt, killed even. And I don't think you want any of that to happen, not from one impulsive gesture that had no real malicious intent, apart from to make me look silly. But sometimes our actions have unforeseen consequences. Anyway, I have an b idea.'

The protestors looked at her questioningly.

'I know there is more to this—if you are here protesting, some of you may be doing it on principle because you want the right to vote for your rulers, have a democracy. Others of you will have other reasons.' She looked at the girl who had thrown the tomato.

'My brother is ill—he has been waiting for a hospital appointment for nine months and he is getting worse. We don't have the money to go private. We have no insurance.'

'And these are all things that should be heard.' Rohan stepped forward now. 'My sister believes that we should hold meetings where people can come to us and tell us of cases like his, matters that need our attention. I will do what I can to make this happen.'

Elora nodded. 'In the meantime, you all have every right to make a peaceful protest.' She turned to Rohan. 'Thank you for listening, thank you for turning round and for asking Security to let us talk.'

Rohan could only admire the way she had somehow contrived to give him credit in public for something she had instigated. But he saw how she stumbled slightly as she turned to walk back to the carriage and knew on some visceral level that she was holding herself together by a thread. He wrapped an arm around her waist, knowing she wouldn't want anyone to suspect that she was struggling. Perhaps it was delayed reaction, though right now he was unsure what, exactly, had caused it.

'That was a good call,' he said, his voice deep

and reassuring as they headed to the waiting carriage and horses, and now he could feel her tension, sense the clench of her muscles, hear the quickening of her breath. 'It's fine,' he murmured. 'We've got this.' He helped her into the carriage and his admiration soared again as he saw her pull herself together, sit straight and tall, a smile on her face as she looked around, but close up he could see her pallor and he knew what to do—the only thing he could think of to do.

He turned to face her. 'Look at me,' he said softly, and she did. 'Trust me?' he asked, and she gave a small nod.

And oh, so gently, he cupped her face in his hands and almost before she realised what he was doing he leaned forward and kissed her, poured his admiration and warmth and reassurance into the kiss. And after a surprised second she responded, the kiss different from their others, though no less passionate. This one held sweetness and a low simmer of heat, building in a gentle crescendo of passion.

Eventually the cheers of the crowd penetrated the fog of desire and in joint consensus they pulled apart and, as they did, he said so only she could hear, 'That was for you, not for the cameras.'

'I know, but we may as well reap the benefits.'

She sat back and he could see that the tension was gone, though he reached out and took her hand in his and held it firmly until they arrived at their destination.

CHAPTER THIRTEEN

ELORA LOOKED DOWN at the hand that clasped hers as the carriage drew to a blessed stop. Registered that his touch had calmed the turmoil inside her, knew that without that kiss she would most likely have baulked at remaining in the carriage, would have shown her anxieties and fears in public. And, worse, to do so would have escalated the situation, brought further attention to an incident that, in truth, was little more than trivial, though the underlying cause for protest was anything but.

'We're here,' Rohan said, and she looked around to see a wrought iron gate set in a stone wall. Peering through, she saw a beautiful lush garden dotted with flowering bushes, exuberant bursts of reds and oranges amongst tall exotic shrubs and trees, verdant with differing hues of green, the spectrum veering from lime to a deep, deep green.

'It's beautiful,' she said as she alighted from the carriage with a sensation of relief and they entered the peaceful, warm atmosphere of the gardens.

'And private. It will be a good place to talk.'

Elora glanced at him. 'Talk?'

'Yes. About what happened back there. I did as you asked without question, I trusted you, and now you need to trust me.'

He made it sound so easy, but trusting him meant sharing things she had never shared before. Yet she did owe him that. He had listened to her, had trusted her in a way no one had ever done before, or at least not since Sanjay. Her brother had trusted her implicitly, as she had trusted him. But Rohan had helped her, allowed her to defuse a situation, possibly avert tragedy, and so, 'You're right. I do owe you an explanation.'

'No, I don't mean that. I want you to trust me, not because you owe me but because you can. I want to help. I want to know.'

She nodded.

'Come, let's walk. There is a pagoda by a lake where we can eat. And talk.'

As they walked she absorbed the sunshine and the scents from the flowers, looked around and saw just how much thought and care must have gone into these grounds.

'So does this belong to the royal family?'

Rohan nodded. 'Yes. We open it to the public regularly throughout the year, but otherwise it is for royal use.'

She was grateful for the small talk and the

companionable silence until they reached their destination, a picturesque blue lake, dotted with wild birds who skimmed the water with movement and colour. Nearby was the promised pagoda, a pretty circular roofed structure which contained a small table and chairs, where they were soon seated.

'You were amazing back there,' Rohan said. 'You defused a situation that could have turned ugly.'

She gave a small hard laugh. 'No. What I did back there was defuse a situation I had created.'

'I don't understand.' Rohan poured a glass of the sparkling mango juice he'd brought and handed it to her and she accepted it gratefully, let the cool, sweet liquid run down her throat as the events of the past hour ran through her head. Anxiety threatened again and she let the warm rays of the sun wash over her, but most of all knew she was taking comfort from Rohan's presence.

She tried to work out the best way to explain and, in the end, settled for the one fact that had impacted her life so much and for so long—the fact that had precipitated tragedy and loss.

'I'm scared of horses,' she said. 'Terrified is a better word.' And she could hear her voice crack with regret and guilt, the thread of sadness and resignation, and Rohan took her hand in his, said nothing, asked no questions, let her take her time.

'I always have been, though I don't know why. On Caruli, horses are an integral part of our culture and tradition. History speaks of kings and princes riding bareback across the island, of brave cavalries that fought battles, of loyal stallions. The royal stable has thoroughbreds with family dynasties of their own, going back hundreds of years. Carulian royalty love horses—it's a given, an important tradition, tied up with so much of our culture. Horses have always been seen as noble creatures. But somehow, from the moment I was taken to the stables, all I felt was terror. Which horrified my parents. Basically, I was told to get over it, that this was not allowed. Once they forced me to stay in a stable with one of the thoroughbreds. There was a groom in there with me and I am sure it was one of the gentler horses, but to me it was like being locked in with a monster.'

She saw anger cross Rohan's face and squeezed his hand. 'I know it sounds cruel and I would never do that to anyone. But to my parents my fear was inexplicable, a flaw in my make-up; they genuinely believed confronting it would cure it and, to a degree, it did. I was so scared they would shut me in again that I managed to learn to control the fear a little bit. I also gained a friend in the groom; he helped allay my fears in there.'

'But you are still terrified inside.'

'Yes, I am. But it was Sanjay who helped back then. He knew of my fear and he helped protect me from it. When he was there I felt safer and because he loved horses, had no fear of them, that helped me.

'But then…' She pulled her hand from his, clenched her hands into the grass, looked away from him, not sure if she could relive the memories, the searing pain and guilt.

'Elora, it's OK. I'm here. You don't have to carry this alone.'

But she did. This was her burden to bear and here and now she needed to face it, acknowledge it, and so she began to speak.

'Sanjay and I were eleven, which is the time for a coming-of-age ritual on Caruli. A time when we were to be given our own horses, entrusted to look after them, as they would look after us. Sanjay was so excited; he already loved the horse that had been chosen for him. He kept telling me it would all be OK, that I just had to get through the ritual, that he would be there. "All" I had to do was mount the horse and ride it through the palace grounds and then through a few of the streets so the public could see.'

'I imagine to the child you were then, that

must have filled you with overwhelming fear. To get on the horse and then ride it alone. In public.' There was no judgement, just understanding, and when he looked at her she felt as though somehow he was reliving the experience with her, could see her as she'd been then, a small, scrawny, terrified little girl with two long blonde plaits, eyes screwed up, wishing, praying, that something—anything would happen to mean she didn't have to go through with it. Well, something had.

'We were in the stable area—Sanjay and me and Jaswant; he was an undergroom back then. Sanjay was on his horse and he was so confident so happy and I was so scared. And I was so full of shame as well, that I was such a coward. I knew I couldn't do it.'

She could recall the fear, the scent of her own sweat, wanting to laugh hysterically because she'd been told that princesses didn't sweat, they perspired. Could feel the scratch of her clothes and see the shining flanks of the horses, sleek and so powerful, so much stronger than her.

'Jaswant had managed to help me onto the horse, but then the horse reared slightly, could sense my fear, and I screamed. Sanjay saw and he wanted to help me.'

She could hear it now, his voice. *'It's OK, Elli, I'm coming.'*

'But for some reason he decided to try and dismount, probably thought bringing his horse over to me would spook me more. His foot somehow got caught in the stirrup and then he got tangled up, lost his balance and slipped, which made the horse bolt and Sanjay fell and hit his head.'

She could still hear the sickening thud.

'It all happened so fast and I was crying and Jaswant somehow kept his head enough to get me off the horse and catch the horses so no one got trampled…and I ran to Sanjay and I didn't know what to do—just prayed and prayed he'd be OK. But he wasn't—he didn't recover and he died two days later.'

She turned now, didn't want to see what would be in Rohan's eyes, but knew she had to.

'It was my fault.'

'No.' His voice was fierce, jagged, and she knew he felt her pain. 'It wasn't. It was a tragic accident, a series of events that culminated in heartbreak. But it was not your fault.'

'If I hadn't screamed, if I had controlled my fear better, or maybe if I'd had the courage to refuse to get onto that horse in the first place, then Sanjay would be alive.'

'You don't know that.' Now he had his arm around her, holding her clasped to his side, and the sheer warmth and strength of his body gave her comfort. 'There are some people who believe the day of your death is set in the stars from the day you are born. It is possible that Sanjay's horse would have bolted regardless, perhaps during the procession. But, regardless of whether you believe that or not, it was a tragic accident and it was not your fault. Though I understand why you must think again and again about the what-ifs and wish you could change what happened.'

She nodded. 'For years I relived it every day. Jaswant never told anyone what had happened, never mentioned that I'd screamed or why Sanjay was trying to dismount. He has never even spoken of it to me. My mother believes it was somehow my fault but she doesn't know the facts.'

'So all these years you've carried this secret, this knowledge. I am so sorry, Elora, so very sorry.'

And now he shifted and he held her, her face against the solid strength of his chest, and for the first time in years she cried, wept and wept until she didn't have any tears left, and only then did he release her.

'So that's what happened today,' she said. 'It was nothing to do with the tomato. Something spooked the horse and it reared. That's why I screamed. It all happened at once. If I hadn't screamed, I doubt we would even have noticed the tomato, but then I was terrified that history would be repeated. That my fear would trigger a chain of events that would end in tragedy. Again.' She managed a smile. 'So thank you for helping me, for trusting me, so that didn't happen.'

'Oh, sweetheart, you don't need to thank me. What you have been through, what you went through today, and yet you acted with courage and good sense and such poise. You are a true princess, Elora.'

'Thank you.' She turned to look up at him and what she saw in his eyes made her gasp, a warmth that touched her to the core, and then, as their gazes meshed, something happened, the warmth changed nuance and sparked into desire, and now...now she was aware of his closeness, his proximity, his strength in a completely different way and awareness began to grow. She felt the rock-hard muscles of his chest and if she shifted that hand the accelerated beat of his heart.

She saw the glint of the sun on the deep black of his hair, the set of his jaw and the firm line of his mouth and now she knew with a glorious sense of inevitability what would happen next and she wanted it, needed it, desired it with every fibre of her.

Then they were kissing and this kiss was different, here, in this place of unspoiled nature, where they were all alone—a place where she'd shared something profound—and all that gave this desire, a depth, a sweetness and a heat and a sharpness that was impossible to resist or even want to resist.

Now their bodies were pressed together and her hands were fumbling, trying to get his T-shirt over his head, whilst not wanting to break the kiss, break the connection, and then it was done and her fingers were trailing over his bare skin, greedy and wondrous at the feel of his response as he pulled her closer, and then she was on top of him and all she knew was that she wanted more.

The ring of his phone pealed through the air and with an impatient noise he tugged it from his pocket and threw it to the ground. Must have pressed a button in so doing as it clicked to voice-mail and there was Marisa's voice. 'Sorry to call, little bro, but I thought you needed to know. Caro called me—she's on her way to Sarala. I'm not sure why, but I couldn't dissuade her...'

The words were more than enough to break the connection that had seemed so all-consuming. Reality seeped in, cold and absolute, and she moved off him, rose to her feet and closed her eyes, rubbed a hand over her face, over her lips, then to her hair in a desperate attempt to undo the past minutes.

Caro.

The name was a reminder that, whilst she had bared her soul, she still knew nothing about Rohan's first marriage, he still had given her no refutation of the events outlined in the press, outlined by Caro—his first wife, the woman he'd once looked at with adoration.

'You'd better call Marisa.' Her voice sounded drained even to her own ears and he shook his head, rose to his feet and moved towards her.

'I will, but not yet. Not until I know you are OK.' He took a deep breath and then another. 'Perhaps it is a good thing we were interrupted. Before we got too carried away. Thank you for your trust in me today; truly, I value it.' Now he stepped forward and kissed her gently, a brief brush over her lips, and then he picked up his discarded phone and moved away from her.

Elora ran a hand over her lips and tried to think, knew she was too tired to do so clearly but questions pinged around her brain. Why was Caro coming back? How did Rohan feel about that? Did she want him back? Foolish thought— this was the woman who had fled from him, denounced him as a cruel husband. Caro. The woman he'd loved. Or so she believed. The woman he wouldn't speak about.

Rohan walked back to her and now his face

was grim, reminiscent of the man she'd first met in the Treasure Room only a week before.

'We'd better get back to the palace. I've asked for a car to come and get us.'

'Thank you.' That was kind of him. 'But we should make sure it is an open-topped one. We should let the people see us—see that Caro's return has not affected us, you and me. Let the people see we stand together.'

He nodded. 'You're right.'

But she could see the wariness in his dark eyes, and perhaps it mirrored her own. Did they stand together? Could they when Caro was here to wreak who knew what damage?

CHAPTER FOURTEEN

ELORA OPENED HER eyes the following morning and felt a sense of foreboding. Since their return to the palace the previous day there had been an unease, a tension, a sense of waiting.

Because that was what they were doing— waiting to see what Caro would do. As the Queen had said, 'There is nothing to do but respond when we see what she does.'

The King had simply said, 'She is old news. She can stir up old news. There is nothing else she can do.'

Marisa had looked at Rohan and said simply, 'It's in your hands, Rohan. My advice is to stand your ground. Caro will be enjoying the idea she's got you on tenterhooks.'

And Rohan… He had said nothing. Elora had no idea what he was thinking and she had decided not to ask, but hurt burned inside her. After what she had shared, after the previous day, she'd believed… Believed what, exactly? That something had changed? That there was a connection beyond the physical?

There wasn't. Or if there was it meant nothing. It was part of an agreement, a contractual marriage of convenience made for political gain. The romance was a charade, and now the test would be whether their woven illusion was strong enough to withstand the advent of Caro.

How was Rohan feeling? Was he looking forward to seeing his first wife again? Did he still love her?

The thought was enough to force her out of bed, though she decided to skip the family breakfast. She would text Marisa to let her know. The thought of sitting in silence, or sitting next to a man who was presumably brooding on another woman, was not conducive to appetite.

Instead, she went down to the palace kitchens, where she'd already befriended the staff, and requested a few pieces of freshly baked bread and a chunk of cheese. Then she set out into the palace gardens, wandered around, before settling on a small wooden bench next to a bush that blazed with bright red blooms.

'Psst! Elora!'

Elora turned her head and frowned, sure she didn't recognise the voice. Unless it was a staff member or Marisa disguising her voice. Hard to imagine Marisa doing that.

She stood up and looked towards where the voice came from, as a woman stepped out from behind the bush.

Elora blinked, wondering if she'd actually hallucinated her into being, but knew she hadn't. The beautiful woman with auburn hair cut into a sleek bob was undoubtedly Caro. The woman who she'd seen so many times on the big screen, admired as an actor for her ability to make every part she played so real, for bringing both beauty and talent to her work. But a woman she'd also seen on the pages of so many magazines, denouncing Rohan.

Caro put a finger to her lips. 'Don't call Security. I persuaded someone to let me in. His teenage son is a fan of mine so I signed an autograph and promised to send him a signed photo as well. Look, I really don't want anyone to get into trouble, and I'm not here to make a scene or cause trouble. I just want ten minutes of your time, that's all.'

Elora weighed up her options. Calling Security seemed pointless and surely would only generate potential negative publicity. Plus she was curious, wanted to know what Caro had to say.

'OK. Ten minutes.'

'Are you escaping the family breakfast? I'm sorry my arrival on Sarala has caused a problem.'

'You must have known it would.'

Caro shrugged elegant shoulders. 'Yes, but I wanted to talk to you.'

'You could have called, could have set up a video conference.'

Caro waved a dismissive hand. 'That isn't the same. I wanted to see you properly, and anyway you can hang up on a call or leave a meeting.'

'Fair enough. So what do you have to say?'

'Don't do it.' Now Caro's voice was low, urgent. 'I married Rohan because I thought he was something he wasn't. I was taken in by his looks and he made me feel as though I was the world to him, but then, once we were married, everything changed. I knew I'd made a massive mistake and I don't want to see you or anyone else do the same. I'm sure you think it will all be OK, that he will be a good husband, but he won't be. He made my life a misery, became a monster, and all I wanted to do was escape. I felt trapped, suffocated—don't make the same mistake I did.'

Her voice cracked, her beautiful face etched with remembered pain. 'Look at me now. I got away and now I'm happy, married to a man I love. Don't give up your chance for that, because *you'll* never be able to leave, he won't let you.' Caro laid a hand on Elora's arm. 'I know the King and Queen… With the situation on Baluka, I know how desperately they will now want Rohan to marry and produce an heir. I know as well how important that will be to him. To do his duty, do the right thing. But you don't need to be taken in, you don't need to sacrifice yourself. You deserve what I have now.'

Elora tried to think, tried to work out what was going on. Caro sounded utterly sincere. Elora would swear that she was telling the truth, or at least the truth as she saw it. What had Marisa said? That Caro created drama and illusions. Perhaps the reason she was such a good actor was her ability to truly believe whatever drama she decided to play out.

But what was she really saying? That *she* had felt trapped, that *she* had made a mistake, that *she* had believed she meant the world to Rohan. That she was happy now in a marriage based on love. But Elora still didn't know Rohan's side and it occurred to her now that no one did. Because he wouldn't tell it. So all Elora could do was work on what she knew of Rohan.

A man who had shown her nothing but honesty and truth even in the illusion they were weaving.

'Caro, thank you for coming here, for telling me all this. But the Rohan I know is different from the Rohan you describe. I trust in him. I cannot believe he will turn into a monster, trap me or suffocate me.'

'But that is what I thought, what I believed.'

'But Elora isn't you.' There was a rustle of leaves as Rohan stepped into view, his face unreadable. 'I apologise. I came to look for Elora. I didn't expect to find you here, Caro.'

'I came to speak to Elora. If you wish to call Security…'

'I don't. If you wish to come into the palace, you and Elora can continue your conversation there or here, or you can come and see my parents and sister. Or anyone else within the palace. You are welcome.' His voice was even.

'Welcome?' Caro's voice held an almost outraged surprise, as if Rohan wasn't playing his ascribed role.

'Yes, you are welcome. Welcome to say what you have come to say, tell the story as you see it.'

Caro hesitated and then shrugged. 'I will go.' She turned back to Elora, her green eyes wide and imploring. 'Please think about what I have said.'

'I will.'

With that, Caro slipped away.

'I will just make sure she really does leave.' A few minutes later, Rohan returned.

'How long were you listening?' Elora asked.

'Just at the end. I really did come to find you, to see why you skipped out on breakfast. Did you mean what you said to her?'

'Yes.' Every word felt weighted right now,

but Elora wanted to speak the truth. 'I wish you would tell your side, but if you won't then all I can do is make a judgement based on my knowledge of you. The person you are now.'

'I will tell my side.'

Elora looked at him warily, relieved when a small smile tipped his lips.

'Don't look so surprised. You showed a trust in me that I am not sure I deserve, but it seems fair to let you be the judge. You've heard some of Caro's side, now I will tell you mine.' He looked around. 'But not here. We are too likely to get interrupted.' He thought for a moment. 'There is an old disused barn out by the orchards. I used to hide out there as a kid. We can go there.'

Half an hour later he'd driven them through the palace grounds and parked outside the barn, led the way in. Let down the ladder leading to the hayloft and gestured to Elora to climb up.

'I can see why this was a good hideout,' she said as she looked around. 'The hay makes it cosy and warm and being up here is really private.'

He nodded. 'It seems like a good place to tell this story.'

They settled by the window, overlooking the orchards, with the palace looming in the distance. She studied his expression, saw no hesitation or regret that he had decided to tell her the truth about his marriage. There was a small frown on his face and she sensed he was marshalling his thoughts.

And then he began. 'When I met Caro I was twenty-three, *I* was the inexperienced, gauche Prince. I'd been out on a few dates, but never a serious relationship, or anywhere near. I'd gone abroad to Europe, my first time away from Sarala on my own, and that's where I met Caro. An actress, a serious actress at that, she'd been acting since she was talent-spotted as a teenager and she'd just had rave reviews for a film. She was only two years older than me in terms of age but about ten years older in experience. She'd left her family home at fifteen to be a model and she'd had a succession of high-profile relationships. Hollywood actors, a French politician, a Formula One driver. And for some reason her attention lit on me. I don't know why. Maybe she wanted to add a prince to her list. But soon we were dating. And I was bedazzled.'

'Of course you were. How could you not be?'

'I didn't know whether I was coming or going and I think that amused her, or perhaps it gave her balm. She'd come out of a messy breakup and there I was, willing to worship and adore her. And soon I asked her to marry me, because back then I thought that was the right, romantic thing to do. I wouldn't have dreamt of sleeping with her first. I wanted to show her I was different. That I had honour.' She could hear the self-mocking tone in his voice, and she could picture him as he had been then, in the throes of first love.

'At first she refused, but then she changed her mind. I don't know why—perhaps it was because she believed that being worshipped, me thinking the world of her, would be enough. Perhaps she wanted the glamour of being a princess, perhaps she thought it would help her career. She said it would be a fresh start, that she would be a princess who the people adored. But I thought she loved me. I was sure I loved her.'

Without thinking, she placed a hand gently over his and, oddly, it felt as though she were walking back through the past with him, that they were watching his younger self trying to navigate the emotional minefields of his first marriage.

'At first everything was blissful. I was completely in her thrall and Caro liked that. And it wasn't just me. She had—has—the ability to charm people, to make people believe they are wonderful. But…it's not real. I'm not sure when I realised it. Perhaps the day she stopped to help up a child, a staff member's daughter who had fallen over. She was loveliness itself. But two days later, when the little girl came to give her flowers, she couldn't really recall who she was, was a bit dismissive, and I saw how hurt the girl was. It wasn't a big thing, but to me it was the start. And soon after that I began to annoy her, and I understand why. I wanted to be with her all the time, wanted to read her poetry, wanted to do things together. And she started wanting her own space, her own time. Which was fair enough, but I didn't understand, took it as rejection. And I noticed her flirting with other men. She'd tell me I was being silly, jealous, but then Marisa noticed it too. And other people—I could see the funny looks, the hidden smiles.'

Elora could only imagine what that would have done to Rohan, how hurt his pride must have been, how confused and miserable and small it would have made him feel. His wife showing favour to other men, people smirking, his own love being repudiated, his romantic gestures met with indifference, labelled annoying.

'So, yes, there were arguments. I ordered, begged, pleaded with her, but she got more and more angry and in the end she went home, back to Europe for a "break". Said perhaps she would see if there were any acting opportunities. And when she came back she was different. I didn't understand it. At first I was pleased because she stopped flirting with other men, but she also stopped wanting to be with me. Started sleeping in a separate room, said she needed some time. I didn't understand, or maybe I didn't want to understand, but things became harder. I could see she didn't want to be with me, but then, suddenly she changed again.'

His face was tired now, weary, the lips set in a grim line, and Elora felt for him, knew these were dark memories that haunted him, understood all too well how that felt.

'Suddenly she was loving again. She asked me out for dinner, took me to a place we'd gone to in the early days, and I was so happy. And then, over dinner, she told me why she'd been strange, explained her behaviour. She told me she was pregnant, that it must have played havoc with her hormones. I was so ecstatic I was going to be a father, we were going to have a baby, and I wanted to shout it from the rooftops, but Caro wouldn't let me. Said she wanted to wait until she was absolutely sure she was safe, but she'd wanted me to know. So of course I agreed not to tell anyone, but then she refused to see a doctor, said there was no need, not yet. Told me not to worry, to be happy. We were having a baby and I was happy, but something still felt off. She still wanted separate bedrooms, didn't even want a hug, but I put it all down to hormones, focused on looking forward to being a dad. And I swear to you, Elora, I didn't care, girl or boy, I was just happy.' He shook his head.

'Anyway, then everything blew up. Caro said she wanted to go back to Europe. I asked if it was safe to fly and she lost the plot, said I was trying to imprison her, and it was soon after that that she tried to flee by night. Even though I had never said she couldn't go. And in the end I found out the truth—the baby wasn't mine.'

'Oh.' Elora stared at him, tried to imagine how that would have felt—the grief of believing you were going to be a father and then finding out you weren't. The searing pain of betrayal, the anger, the sadness, the whole gamut of emotions.

'She'd met someone when she was back in Europe, a director, but then he had rejected her so she decided to try to make me believe the baby was mine. That's why she didn't want to go to the doctor—in case it was obvious that she was less pregnant than she had claimed, but as time went on she believed she could wing it. Fudge the issue. But now the man had changed his mind, wanted her back. So I said she could go as long as she told no one about the man or the baby. I couldn't bear the humiliation or all the rumours, the DNA testing. So we divorced.'

'And you let the press rip into you, paint you as a monster. Why?'

'Because that was preferable to the truth. And

it was better for the baby. Caro left and soon after she announced her new romance. They went travelling, she said she wanted to be left alone and then she had her baby, a home birth, and no one ever thought to question the timing because by then she and her husband were married and she was busy spinning other stories. Now they have another child and they are a happy family. Caro is acting again and she has it all.' He shrugged his shoulders. 'So there you have it.'

Now, finally, she felt she could speak. 'I'm sorry…so, so sorry. To believe you were going to be a father and then to find out you weren't. To have been betrayed on that deep a level—that goes beyond unfaithfulness. I know you don't want to speak of it but I'm still sorry you had to go through it.'

'That was hardest of all. Caro being unfaithful— yes, that hurt, but it hurt my pride. By then, I think I knew she'd never loved me. I don't think I ever loved her, not really. I loved the idea of loving her but, when it came to it, we never really knew each other. But when I thought I was going to have a baby, that was love…'

'And when that was taken from you, you were angry, but mostly you were grieving.'

'Yes. But now, telling you this, sharing it, you trusting me, me trusting you, I feel lighter. As though this is the foundation for our future, we will have a marriage based on trust and soon, hopefully very soon, we will be married and...' He grinned at her, and suddenly he looked lighter, younger. 'Hopefully, soon we will have a baby, a family.'

The words hit Elora like a punch in the gut. Rohan was talking about trust—mutual trust being the bedrock, the foundation of their union. And now she knew something she hadn't known before—that Rohan had already once been cheated of a baby, a family. Knew that this man wanted children, didn't care if they were sons or daughters. His words at the temple, sworn in a sacred place, had shown her that.

She was a fraud, and how could she let this man enter another union based on a lie, believing it was based on trust? For a long moment she looked at him, took in his masculine beauty, relived the feel of his lips against hers, their bodies pressed against each other, the glorious feel of his naked chest under her fingers, the sheer level of want and need and desire between them. Remembered too the way he'd held her as she'd cried, how he'd listened, how he'd engaged with her idea. Remembered the walk through the spice market, sitting by the temple, and she knew she was processing and storing those memories before she did what she had to do.

Knew too, with a sudden blinding clarity, that

she loved him, loved the prince who had somehow, somewhere captured her heart. A heart that
she could feel cracking inside her even as her
brain made one last-ditch attempt to consider
the arguments her mother had deployed, that she
herself had deployed over the past days to justify
a decision she'd known all along to be wrong.
Thought now too of what her mother would say
to her, the venomous hiss of vitriol and bitter displeasure, her father's weary resignation, another
notch of disappointment on the list.

But it didn't change anything.

'We need to talk,' she said slowly.

CHAPTER FIFTEEN

THERE WAS A moment of silence as Rohan studied Elora's face. Perhaps she should look incongruous here amongst the hay bales, but she didn't. She just looked beautiful. And sad. And determined. And he had a sudden feeling of foreboding.

'I thought we were talking.'

'We are, and what you have shared with me… I appreciate more than I can tell you. I understand how hard it is to trust.'

Of course she did. She had spent the past decade and more keeping the circumstances of her brother's death a secret, unable to trust her parents or the people who should have been there for her.

'And that's why I can't go ahead with this marriage—our marriage.'

The words were so unexpected he simply froze and then in a delayed reaction they hit him, a missile he hadn't seen coming.

'Why? Is it something Caro said?'

She shook her head. 'It's what I haven't said.'

She clenched her nails into her hands and then faced him, her grey eyes unwavering. 'There is a chance, a good chance, that I may have fertility problems. That there won't be a baby.'

'I… I don't understand.'

'My mother struggled to have a baby. In the end she had IVF treatment. No one knew—she went abroad to receive it. That resulted in Sanjay and me. It is possible that I have inherited her issues, though there is a lot that isn't known about inherited fertility problems. But it's more than that. My periods are irregular, patchy, and always have been. That makes it harder to conceive.'

She delivered each fact straight, no quaver in her voice, and as the import of her words hit him he could feel anger surge in his gut, cold and bleak, as he realised how close he'd come to being taken for a ride, conned again.

'Why are you only mentioning this now?' He could hear the ice in his voice as he moved away from her.

'Because when I wanted to at first my mother told me not to.' She raised a hand. 'I know that sounds ridiculous but…'

But he understood the influence, the power, Queen Joanna wielded.

'And I believed her reasons, thought they had validity. She told me not to create problems where they don't exist, that my periods are down

to my foolish anxieties that can and will be over-
come, that this marriage was vital for Caruli and
that was what mattered. And so I put my doubts
aside, told myself she was right.'

Rohan tried to think, but right now all he
could see was the fact that Elora had not told
him the full truth.

'And this week, when we discussed having
children, when it must have become increasingly
clear to you that Sarala needs an heir, that this is
the duty I have chosen to embrace...' However
heavy it was, however much he didn't want it,
but the saving grace was having a child, a family. 'What was your plan if a child didn't come?'

'I had no plan,' she said. 'I just had hope.' Now
she showed a flash of spirit. 'After all, do you
know that you can have children?'

'No. But I have no reason to believe that I can't.'

'Touché. I deserved that. But when we first
met I didn't know you. I didn't want to marry
you, but I knew I had to. I thought that perhaps
I was making excuses, looking for a reason to
not do it. And then, each day that passed...' for
the first time she paused, stared at him with eyes
wide '...it became harder to tell you, so I buried
my head in the sand. I was wrong and that's why
I am releasing you from our agreement.'

'It's not that easy.' And it wasn't. 'We've spent
a week spinning a mythical romance. How are

we supposed to end it? We kissed in public, we've been on dates, we've made it clear we are an item. If we end it now, it will look as though either we have been playing them all along or that Caro has influenced your decision.' The anger was heightening now, but he recognised it was two-pronged—he was angry because he didn't want to end the agreement, felt doubly cheated because the idea of no marriage when he'd found the perfect partner, the person he wanted to marry, a woman he… He slammed the thought to a halt. A woman he had been dealing with in good faith, a woman who hadn't dealt fairly with him, and yet…as he looked at Elora, he knew he didn't want this to end.

'I know. But I will take the blame.'

'No.' Now his voice was cold. 'We cannot end the charade as yet. We will have to continue the pretence, the illusion, until a better time.'

'I… I don't know if I can do that.'

'There is no choice. It will give us time to work out a strategy, a way to tell our parents. Your mother…' Whatever fault lay with Elora, she didn't deserve the backlash.

Elora shook her head. 'It doesn't matter. What I did was wrong, Rohan. I didn't do what I knew was right because I thought you wouldn't go ahead with the marriage. I know how ugly that sounds. But I wanted to show my parents that I could do something for Caruli, could earn some redemption.'

And, just like that, his anger dissipated. He understood why she had done what she had and he stepped forward, but stopped when she shook her head.

'Don't.' She managed a smile. 'I'll just cry. Because somehow, over these past days, I did believe we had a chance.'

'Maybe we still do. Maybe we should go ahead, marry anyway. Take the risk.'

'We can't.' Her voice was rock steady now. 'I've seen what it's like, what the desperation to have an heir can do. It would tear us apart and it's not fair on you. You are already sacrificing your dream, your company, what you want to do with your life, to do your duty. I can't make it harder for you, can't take that risk. You can't. Tell me the truth, Rohan. If I had told you from the start, wouldn't you have thought the risk too high? Wouldn't your parents and Marisa agree? Your sister would tell you that you have to do what is best for Sarala, and that isn't me. I'm potentially damaged goods.'

He broke off, closed his eyes, tried to think straight. What did he want? The answer was instant and true. He wanted Elora.

But Elora was right. Sarala needed an heir. Elora might not be able to provide one.

Or she might.

But the risk was too great.

And this wasn't all about him. What about Elora? What did she want? For her. Not for Caruli, not for her parents, not for a mother who didn't deserve a daughter like Elora, or a father for whom the need for an heir had overridden all else. She wanted a normal life, so perhaps, unbelievably, Caro had been right. Elora deserved what Caro had, a man to love her for herself, who could give her that normal life she craved. Relative anonymity where she could perhaps be more like Preeti Bannerjee than Princess Elora.

And that meant he needed to do the right thing.

He wouldn't condemn Elora to a life of being watched, the pressure of becoming pregnant, that monthly question with the eyes of the world upon them. Wouldn't subject her to blame if there was no child—or a daughter.

The Prince of Sarala would do the right thing for Sarala and for Elora.

'You're right. Our marriage is not possible, but we *will* need to continue the charade a little longer. But for now we will come up with a reason for you to return to Caruli. Perhaps we can say, or imply that I don't wish you to be subjected to Caro, or hurt in any way. So I will take you back and then return to Sarala alone. We will then let our romance "fizzle out".'

He could hear the coldness in his voice but he knew that was the only way he could do this, the only way he could go through with it. When every particle of his being wanted to tell her that it didn't matter, they'd take the risk.

Elora nodded. 'I…hope that things work out. I hope that somehow, some way, you can keep your company, at least partially realise your dreams. And when you do marry, I promise I wish you all the best and I hope with all my heart that you get the family you want and Sarala needs. I know you will be a good ruler and a wonderful dad. Thank you for the past week. I mean that. And Rohan, I'm sorry. I truly am.'

Five days later

Rohan sat outside the temple, tried to think about his grandfather, grey-haired and still upright even in his eighties. Remembered the last time the old man had brought him here.

'I have lived a long time, Rohan, and yet my whole life has been dedicated to Sarala, as yours will be too.'

A pause, and then, as if there was no connection…

'Marisa is a clever girl; she too loves her country. As my sisters did.'

His grandfather had been the fourth child and

first and only son of his parents and, sitting here now, Rohan wondered what the old King had been thinking back then. Whether he had ever entertained the enormity of thought that was in Rohan's mind now.

Wondered too what Elora would think.

Elora… He could picture her so clearly, as if she were branded on his brain, just as he was beginning to believe she was branded on his very heart and soul. Because, however hard he tried to not think about her, she was always there. Waking and sleeping, she haunted his dreams and, wherever he was, the scent of jasmine, the taste of cumin, the glimpse of a woman dressed in teal…any little thing brought back a memory.

He'd like to have spoken with her about his decision but he knew in the end this decision was his and his alone. Enough pressure had been put on Elora to make decisions based on duty and sacrifice. He wouldn't speak with her until the dice were rolled and the game played out.

He turned as he heard the familiar footsteps of his sister.

'Hey, little bro, here I am, as requested.' Her voice was gentler than usual as she sat down next to him and he studied her face, almost as if he were seeing his sister for the first time.

'Hey. Thanks for coming.'

'No problem.' She eyed him for a moment. 'Is

this about Elora?' She didn't even wait for an answer. 'Because if it's not, it should be. I don't know what you've done but, whatever it is, go fix it.'

'Excuse me.'

'For years I've felt bad. I knew Caro—I asked her to keep an eye on my little brother for me when he went to Europe for the first time. Look what happened.'

'You tried to stop me from marrying her,' Rohan pointed out.

'You didn't listen to me then. I'm hoping you'll listen to me now. I have never seen you as miserable as you have been these past days, not even during the divorce. I think whatever happened with Caro hurt your pride. I think Elora has broken your heart. You have moped about, barely exchanging a civil word with anyone, but your eyes, Rohan. They are racked with sadness and pain. So my advice is to do something about it. If you've been a fool, go and grovel and hope she'll take you back.'

Rohan stared at his sister and gave a rueful smile. 'I thought I was hiding my feelings.'

'You weren't.'

'So your advice. Is that personal advice or political advice? Do you think I should go and get Elora back for Sarala's sake?'

Now it was Marisa's smile that was rueful. 'It is a bonus that it will help Sarala,' she said.

Rohan inhaled deeply. 'Well, I have an idea that I think will really help Sarala,' he said.

One week later

Elora stared at her reflection, tried to somehow put some sort of smile on her face, a sparkle in her eyes, but for the first time that she could remember she couldn't. Missing Rohan was like a physical ache, one that no ability to act could help. But somehow, from somewhere, she had to find the Princess Elora façade to hide behind. Didn't want anyone to guess the truth—that she had somehow fallen for a man who didn't love her back, had succumbed to a love that could go nowhere, had no hope.

So somehow she had to find some inner strength, a way to face the world, when the news broke that the romance was over. She couldn't continue to hide in her room for ever, though that was exactly what she had been doing the past twelve days. Acting on Rohan's suggestion that they buy some time whilst Caro was in Sarala, whilst they worked out how to announce the breakup, saying she had come down with a bad case of flu, she had returned to Caruli. In the meantime, large bouquets of flowers, bunches of Saralan grapes and two beautiful silk scarves had arrived as gifts with all appropriate fanfare.

The press was, thankfully, distracted by Caro, covering a story of her dining with the Saralan republic party leader, but there were also pictures of a lunch with Marisa. There was speculation that Elora's 'illness' was to avoid confrontation, but the stories were on the whole sympathetic to all parties. And Elora had stayed in her room, tried hard to be strong, do all the right things, whilst inside she was sure she could feel her heart breaking.

And soon they would have to tell the world what she had already told her parents—that it was over.

There was a knock at the door and she looked up. 'Come in.'

The door opened to show Flavia, holding a box. 'Hey.'

'Hey.'

Flavia had been incredible over the past days— had asked no questions, had just been there. They had talked about the past, about Viraj, about Caruli, but Flavia hadn't spoken of her marriage and Elora hadn't spoken of Rohan.

Flavia handed the box over. 'Viraj and I made chocolate chip cookies. And, just so you know, I let him eat the cookie dough.'

'Good.' Elora managed a semblance of her real smile at the thought of her nephew, even as it reminded her of Rohan, the way he'd brought fun into his life. Another reminder of why he deserved the chance to have a family of his own.

And she couldn't help it, an image of Rohan holding a baby, looking down on the infant with pride and joy, filled her mind and then, to her own horror, tears began to spill from her eyes.

'Elora...' In an instant her older sister was by her side, holding her close. 'It's OK.' Her voice was soothing, almost as if Elora were Viraj, and after a few moments Elora gulped to a stop and moved gently away. 'I'm sorry, Flav...'

'Don't be sorry. It's good to let it all out. Is it Rohan?'

As she spoke, she handed Elora a tissue and Elora wiped her eyes and sighed. 'Yes,' she admitted.

'What happened? I know you said it was a mutual decision not to marry. But I thought maybe it was something to do with Caro.'

Elora shook her head. 'Caro tried to warn me off but I told her I trusted Rohan. But then... now... I love him, Flavia, and I've messed it all up and he'll never love me and he's going to marry someone else and...I am so miserable.'

'Whoa. Hold on, Elora. Does he know you love him?'

'No! And there is no way I am telling him.'

'Why not?'

The simple question floored her as she opened her mouth to answer but found no words would come.

Eventually, she said, 'Because there is no point. It's not his fault. He never offered me love or the prospect of it. Just a dutiful marriage. And now that wouldn't be fair to him.'

Flavia thought for a moment. 'Rohan is a good man, I think. I saw how he looked at you. I saw how protective he was of you when your mother treated you badly. Also, I saw him with Viraj— and that spoke volumes for his character. I think a man like Rohan maybe deserves to know that he is loved.'

Before Elora could answer, her phone pinged. 'It's from Rohan.' She scanned the message.

Elora, I need to speak with you. If you agree, I will send a friend of mine to collect you from the airfield tomorrow morning at about eleven o'clock. No need for secrecy, but preferably no fanfare or undue publicity.

'He wants to see me.' She looked at her sister. 'Presumably, he wants to discuss the best way of ending the relationship. Presumably also without fanfare and undue publicity.' The thought filled her with a bleakness that she knew was etched on her face.

'Will you go?'

'Yes.' She knew she couldn't pass up the chance to see him one more time, however much it hurt. 'I want to make sure this time there is no adverse publicity for him.'

'Think about what I said.' Flavia's brown eyes looked suddenly filled with sadness. 'Love is a precious thing.' She moved forward and gave Elora a hug. 'Whatever you decide, good luck.'

Rohan glanced at his watch for what felt like the millionth time in the past five minutes, and wondered how time could crawl so slowly. But she would be here any minute now, any second now, and there went his phone.

Amit, telling him that they had landed.

'She's amazing, Ro. I'm not sure what's going on, but don't let this one go.'

'Thank you, and your advice is duly noted.' Problem one: he didn't think 'this one' would want to stay. He headed towards the plane, aware that his heart was alternating between skipping and pounding; his pulse rate must be irregular enough to cause a doctor concern.

Then he saw her walking down the steps towards him, the elegance, the grace and the wariness all so familiar. His chest ached with the sheer happiness of seeing her again, even if he knew this might be the start of their final time together. He set his jaw. Not if he had anything to do with it.

'Elora, thank you for coming.'

'It seemed necessary and Amit was a charming companion. I was glad to meet him.' And for a second her smile, her true smile, dimpled. 'He told me about the time you and he did a midnight kitchen raid and mistook the flour for the sugar.'

'It made for an interesting cup of coffee,' Rohan conceded, knowing that Amit must have really liked Elora.

As if recalling why she was here, or at least why she thought she was here, Elora's smile disappeared and she looked around.

'So where shall we go to talk?'

'Just over here. But before we do, I want to give you something.'

CHAPTER SIXTEEN

'GIVE ME WHAT?'

'Come this way.' He led the way over to a small paddock and made a gesture. 'If I've got this wrong then please just tell me and there will be no offence taken.'

She stared into the field for a moment, tried to compute what her eyes were seeing. In the corner, contentedly munching at some grass, there was a pony—a sturdy, medium-sized, compact pony.

'This is Elsie,' he said. Now he sounded hesitant. 'She's eight years old and she needs a new home. I know she is a horse but, by definition, she is a small horse and in temperament she is nothing like Carulian horses. I thought she may help—that perhaps getting used to a small, placid horse would be helpful. I spoke with a few therapists and they said usually they would take it a little slower, start with pictures of horses, but seeing as you are already managing to ride horses and be around them, despite your fears, they thought this may be a good idea, as long as you take it slow.' His voice trailed off. 'But if you are looking at Elsie and thinking you want to run a mile, then we'll jettison the idea.'

Elora stared at the pony then looked up at Rohan and she couldn't help it, couldn't hold it back, felt a tear rest on her eyelash, before it dropped to fall down her cheek.

'Hey, I didn't mean to make you cry.'

'I'm not.' She blinked fiercely. 'It's just such a lovely thought.' The first time anyone had tried something positive to help her. 'Can I meet her? I mean, maybe not actually go into the field with her, but if you could get her to come to the gate, and I stand back, then I think I'd be OK.'

Rohan instantly pushed the gate open and she couldn't help it, her gaze caught and lingered on the muscled swell of his arm under the white T-shirt he wore, swept down the lean sinew of his forearm, and now desire entered the mix, simmered in her gut, somehow warmed by what he'd done.

Minutes later, he was leading Elsie over, nice and slow, and he stopped a little way away. 'Well?'

'So far, so good,' she said and she meant it. Somehow, seeing Rohan standing beside the pony helped; she could see the differences between Elsie and the royal horses but she could also see the similarities. The pony was still strong, still had large teeth—was still a horse.

But when Elsie shook her head and then looked straight at Elora her brown eyes seemed friendly and she knew with every fibre of her being that if Rohan was gifting her Elsie then Elsie was safe.

And that gave her the courage to step closer. She was rewarded by a small whinny and she smiled, a real genuine smile, because this felt like a significant step.

'Thank you. Truly. This feels…like it may really help. A step in the right direction.' Almost as if he had somehow read her mind. It was one of the things she had determined in the past two weeks. 'Because I want to try to manage this anxiety better, not hide it and hope for the best, not simply get through each time I have to ride. I want to see if I can get to a point where I am no longer afraid. Or at least less afraid. So thank you. And I am sure Jaswant will help me with the pony.'

'He will. I took the liberty of speaking with him about housing Elsie in the Carulian stables and whether that would be possible. He said yes.'

'Thank you.' And she meant it, though there was a tiny bit of her—OK, a large part of her—that wished, somehow, she and Rohan could have Elsie, that he could be the person to help her, that they were in this together. Because somehow, imperceptibly, right now, that was how it felt.

But that wasn't how it was and it was time to find out why she was really here. 'Truly. To do this for me is so incredibly thoughtful and that's one of the reasons I…'

She broke off, horrified by what she'd been about to say.

Next to her, Rohan stilled, looked down at her, and there was something in his dark brown eyes, something she couldn't read, couldn't identify.

'You what?' he asked. 'That is one of the reasons you…?'

Flavia's words came to her and suddenly the decision was easy.

'I love you,' she said simply. 'I didn't mean to tell you and I didn't mean for it to happen, but I love you. I love you because you are a good man, a kind, strong man who deserves to be loved. I know you don't love me, know you never promised me love, and I know it doesn't change anything. But there it is.'

'You love me?' he asked.

She stepped closer, reached up to touch his cheek. 'Please don't feel bad; I don't. I wouldn't change the past weeks. They've changed me and made me a better person.'

Now a smile lit up his face and as she made to move back he took her hands in his.

'Feel bad? I don't feel bad. I feel…ecstatic. Because *I* love *you*.' He raised a hand and his smile grew, his eyes alight with a sincerity she couldn't question. 'And no, I am not just saying it. That was one of the things I wanted to tell you. Today. That I love you. I promise you, Elora. I love you with all my heart. And I'm a man of my word, remember?'

He was, and she knew he was speaking the truth, knew he wouldn't lie. That wasn't Rohan's way.

'After our conversation, after your return to Caruli, I missed you so much it hurt,' he said. 'And I knew then that I loved you. That I didn't care about the fertility risk, or whether we have boys or girls or any children at all. I just want you. Just you. Elora. Not the Princess of Caruli. You. It's entirely personal, nothing to do with your island or mine.'

'Why didn't you tell me?' she asked, and now reality began to seep in. Was he about to tell her that love was irrelevant, that it didn't change their duty? 'You said you had something else to tell me,' she remembered.

He nodded, kept her hand securely in his. 'Yes.' He took a deep breath. 'Is it OK if we walk and talk? I'd like for you to see this bit of land.'

She looked around, wondered why he'd chosen it. It was a large expanse of rough land, overgrown with grass and wild flowers and the occasional bush.

'Of course.'

'Right. Well, I did a lot more thinking and…
I have stood down as heir to Sarala.'

'What?' Elora tried to absorb the enormity of
his words—understand and take on board the
fact that Rohan had decided to turn destiny on
its head. 'But then who will become heir?'

'Marisa.' He said it simply. 'She is more than
able to take on the role and by rights it should be
hers. She is the elder. And that is right.'

'But whose idea was it?' She turned wide eyes
to him. 'You didn't do it for me, did you? Give
up your birthright?'

'No, I didn't do it for you. I love you and I
would have asked you to marry me and rule by
my side regardless and I believe we would have
made it work because of the strength of our love.'

'Then why?'

'I stepped down because I truly believe it is
the right thing to do. It wasn't an easy decision
to make.' His voice was deep, serious.

'I wish I'd been here. I wish you'd told me.'

He shook his head. 'This had to be my decision and mine alone. I couldn't put the burden on anyone else. But Elora, you were in my
thoughts—you are the one who helped show me
my way, my path.'

'How?'

'We decided that we couldn't risk getting married in case you couldn't have children, even though we didn't know for sure, one way or another. Because I need a male heir. That is wrong. We had other conversations about having daughters. About your father divorcing his wife to get a male heir when he had a daughter. That is wrong. Your mother wishing it had been you instead of Sanjay who died because he was the male heir. That is wrong. Flavia, unable to rule, only worthy to produce a male heir. My sister, older than me but not able to be heir because of her sex. Wrong again. The bottom line is Marisa would make a better ruler than me and she is older, and yet here we were, bound by tradition and history when we were supposed to be modernising the royal family. What was modern about any of what I have described?'

'Not a lot,' Elora said.

'It suddenly seemed crystal-clear what needed to be done. So I did it. Of course, if Marisa had said she didn't want to rule, well, then there'd have been a different problem, but she didn't.'

'But your parents—what did they say?'

Elora was so caught up in the story she only now realised that, somehow, they had come to a halt and were sitting, backs against a tree, right next to each other, reminiscent of their conversation under the mango tree weeks before.

'They didn't want to listen at first, but when

they saw I was adamant, when I pointed out the number of times they took Marisa's advice, and when they knew I was standing down no matter what—they came on board. The past week has been about looking at the legal side, making it all watertight and working out how to make the announcement in the next few weeks. Marisa has gone away for a bit, to be out of the limelight until it is all sorted. And to have some time to herself before her life changes.'

'So now all I have to offer you is me. Not a kingdom to rule, not the chance to be the mother of a ruler. Just me. Rohan.' He shifted away from her. 'If that changes anything I understand. I know our marriage for you was a way to earn your parents' love and redemption. I can't offer you that any more. There is no reason I can give you to be with me now. Except love.'

'And that is the most precious thing you can offer me,' she said softly, her heart bursting with joy, with the knowledge that Rohan loved her, this prince of men, this man who could turn her insides to mush, this man who amidst the turmoil of renouncing a kingdom had found time to get a pony for her—a man who had changed her for ever. He loved her. 'And that is what I offer you back. I love you, Rohan. I fell in love with you, not your title. I fell in love with the man who has been honest with me, a man who trusted me and made me trust him, a fearless man who wanted to stand up for me but also encouraged me to stand up for myself. A man who has bought me a pony to help me fight my fears. You haven't just listened; you've done something about it. You made me feel as though I am worth something.'

With that, he rose and pulled her to her feet and into the biggest possible hug. 'Elora you are worth so much, you are so brave and strong. You've lived your life with a near intolerable burden of guilt and with parents who do not deserve you and you have come out of it without bitterness, able to smile and care, truly care about people. To have the courage to stand up for your convictions and look to help people who need it. You've helped me more than I can ever say, allowed me to trust, to love, to be brave enough to do what is right, and brave enough to want to live my dream. With you.'

He smiled at her, a smile so carefree and light and happy, and she knew it matched the one on her face.

'I have spoken to Marisa and I thought I could run my company, but for the good of Sarala. This land we are on now, my company is going to develop into a resort; it will bring jobs to Sarala, and I will be involved in the designing, building…everything as well as promoting Sarala.

And I want the profits to be ploughed back into the country, to help alleviate poverty, improve medical facilities. And if you want to be involved you can, but I respect that your dream is different, to have an allotment, and that is fine with me.'

Elora laughed and he looked at her with a question in his eyes.

'That dream—it's not valid any more. You've changed that dream. You see, now I believe I can make a difference, that I can be a princess and I can make my dream bigger. I don't have to be Preeti Bannerjee. I can be Princess Elora and I want to be part of your dream and I want you to be part of mine. I want to help, I want to make sure all those profits go to the right causes. Perhaps we can build a new facility. I have also contacted Michel, the chef, and we are in discussion about writing a cookbook together, and again the profits will go to good causes. And in this marriage of ours we will always share our dreams. And one of my dreams is to have a family, but now...'

'Now there is no pressure. We can take our time. We can adopt. We will have a family, Elora, and I know how happy we will be. We are going to have the romance of a lifetime. And every single bit of it will be true.'

She smiled at him. 'All we will have to do is be ourselves.'

And she knew that they would be the happiest people in the world. Elora and Rohan. As themselves. No illusion, no charade, just the reality of a love that would fill her heart for ever.

* * * * *

*Look out for the next story in
the Royal Sarala Weddings duet*

Bound by Their Royal Baby

*And if you enjoyed this story,
check out these other great reads
from Nina Milne*

Snowbound Reunion in Japan
Wedding Planner's Deal with the CEO
Consequence of Their Dubai Night

All available now!